ODDS &

AMULET BOOKS · NEW YORK

AMY IGNATOW

ABRAMS The Art of Books
195 Broadway, New York, NY 10007
abramsbooks.com

To Susan Van Metre and Maggie Lehrman, who
know all my deepest, darkest, secretest grammar mistakes

As you can see, we have a brand-new science lab that Auxano generously donated to the school. Isn't it wonderful? And soon we'll be breaking ground on the tech center.
How wonderful. Is Auxano funding that as well?
Yes, we're so fortunate. And oh, here's one of our top testers now!
Izaak!
Whud I do?
Oh, Izaak. Such a cutup.

The Muelle

Deborah Read Middle School High Achievers Receive Scholarships

In a pleasant surprise for the state's highest test scorers, the Auxano Foundation has granted summer scholarships to Jay Carpenter, Michael Donovan, Claire Jones, Emma Lee, Izaak Marcus, Eric Mathes, Farshad Rajavi, and Siouxsie Rudikoff. The lucky scholars will have the opportunity to spend their summer break working with some of the finest scientific minds in central Pennsylvania.

"We're so pleased!" said Dr. Miryam Ra-javi, mother of Farshad Rajavi, who happens to be a researcher at Auxano Labs. "And I'm looking forward to having lunches with him while we're both working here! Not every day, of course, because I don't want him to be embarrassed."

When asked about the summer opportu-nity, most of the students seemed noncha-lant. "I mean, of course they want us to work for them," high scorer Izaak Marcus said, "we're really smart and stuff."

"I'm hoping they'll give us free reign over our own lab," Jay Carpenter said, visibly very excited. "There's no telling what sort of sci-entific breakthroughs we might make."

There will be a congratulatory banquet held this evening for the kid geniuses at the Auxano campus banquet hall, with Princi-pal Maureen Jacobs, Mayor Rick Wilkins, and Auxano CEO Bork Bork Bork. "We're so proud of our scholars," Principal Jacobs said, "and we can't wait to see what they'll do next!"

THE DAILY WHUT?

Does anyone find it odd that not one, not two, but eight students from Deborah Read are among the top students in the state? Riiiiiight. I once saw some kids in this town and they are not that bright. I once saw some kids trying to steal the enormous inflatable canvas bear above Melody's Sandwich Shoppe. It was bolted down with steel cables. COME. ON.

Now, I'm not saying that every Read student is dumb as a stump. I'm sure that one or two of them have managed the subtle art of breathing through their noses. But eight? EIGHT? Either a huge mistake has been made or there is some shady business happening in Muellersville. Is it so difficult to believe that Principal Jacobs and the parents that happen to work for Auxano would go above and beyond the norm to give their dumb kids an academic advantage?

When your intrepid investigative blogger was in middle school the kids thought it was funny to give other kids swirlies (putting a kid's head in a toilet and flushing it). Most kids are just not smart. Am I the only one who sees this?

Ever questioning,

The Hammer

_____

FARSHAD!" HIS MOTHER CALLED. "COME DOWNSTAIRS to talk to your *mâdarbozorg*!"

"Mom, I'm busy!"

Farshad Rajavi wasn't really busy, but it was the fifth time she'd called him to talk to a relative on the phone since the exam results came back. He'd already spoken to his aunt and uncle in New Jersey, his other aunt in England, his cousin in Texas, his mother's college roommate in California, and now his grandmother was on the phone from Iran. He was pretty sure his conversation with her would be just like the others. "Congratulations, Farshad, we are so proud of you, you are so famous . . ." Maybe if things had been different he might have actually enjoyed the conversation (well, maybe not with his mother's college roommate—that was never not going to feel awkward), but he was too preoccupied with worrying over exactly how he had achieved such a high score on the exam. Was he actually smart, or had Dr. Deery's formula managed to increase his IQ in the same way that it helped that dum-dum Izaak Marcus to get an equally high score? And if he was so smart, he probably could have found a way to break Mr. Friend out of Auxano's prison. He was also nervous about accidentally crushing his mom's cell phone by holding it too hard with his thumb.

"Farshad, you come down here right now!" His mom

was using her DO IT NOW voice. Farshad trudged down the stairs and gently took the phone from his mom's outstretched hand.

COOKIE PARKER WAS LYING ON HER BED NOT answering her texts. She was not answering her texts because, technically, she hadn't received any texts, but that was beside the point; the point was that if she were to receive any texts, she had already made the decision that she would not be answering them. She needed to think.

Thinking, of course, wasn't as easy as it once was. Before the accident she took for granted her ability to think without having the incredibly boring but loud thoughts of others popping into her head, and now she couldn't concentrate because her stepdad was downstairs making Jell-O and concentrating reeeeeeeeaaal hard on what was quite possibly the easiest set of directions she could think of.

Boil water.

Empty packet of Jell-O into bowl.

Pour one cup of hot water into bowl.

Stir.

Add one cup of room temperature water to mixture.

Refrigerate.

Pretty simple, right? But George was thinking, *Uh, okay, need a measuring cup. Can I use a large measuring spoon or do I need the glass thing with the spout? But where is that? I know I saw it somewhere at some point. I'll just use the measuring spoon. But it's plastic. Should I be putting boiling-hot water into plastic? Is it going to melt on me? Maybe I shouldn't boil the water all the way. Maybe it should just be warm water? No, the directions say hot water, not warm water . . .*

Cookie couldn't even be that mad because the only reason her stepfather was making Jell-O in the first place was because she'd made the mistake of telling him that she wasn't feeling very good, and to George "not feeling very good" meant: KID NEED JELL-O. Fever? NEED JELL-O. Scraped knee? NEED JELL-O. Friends not texting? NEED JELL-O. Sudden onset of mind-reading abilities caused by a spilled mystery chemical during a bus accident? NEED JELL-O.

(Not that George knew about her newfound ability to read minds—only when people were thinking about directions—but still, she had said she wasn't feeling well, so, yeah, NEED JELL-O.)

Given that George's answer to every medical problem was Jell-O, Cookie would have thought he'd be better at actually making Jell-O.

Ugh, George, she thought. *The glass measuring cup is in the second cabinet with the mixing bowls and the other baking stuff.*

Oh! There it is. Now, where's the teakettle?

On the stove, doofus, Cookie thought.

Right, on the stove!

Cookie stifled a short gasp. George could hear her thoughts! Was that possible? It was bad enough that she had to listen to his brain try to figure out the intricacies of Jell-O making, but if he could hear her, was nothing she thought private? Was he reading her thoughts RIGHT NOW?!?

Cookie ran down the stairs and grabbed her sweatshirt on the way to the front door.

"Cookiepuss?" George asked as she speed-walked by him. "Where are you going?"

"I . . . uh . . . out."

"But you said you weren't feeling well. I'm making Jell-O!"

Don't think. Don't think. "I was just thinking that some fresh air would do me good. I'll be back by the time the Jell-O is . . . less liquidy." Cookie headed out the door, leaving a befuddled George holding a teakettle in one hand, a glass measuring cup in the other.

**D**ID YOU SEE IT?" JAY CARPENTER SHOVED A LAPTOP into Nick Gross's face. It was Nick's aunt's laptop and he was pretty sure that if Jay broke it Jilly would break him. His aunt was short and extremely pregnant, but she was also pretty strong, and Nick suspected that she wouldn't mind the excuse to hurl Jay into oncoming traffic. A lot of people felt that way about his best friend. Nick was used to it.

"Jay," Nick said, trying not to sound too exasperated (not that Jay would have noticed), "it's hard to read something that's being shoved directly into my face."

"Right-o." Jay took a step back and with a flourish placed the laptop on the coffee table in front of Nick. A tab was opened to a *Daily Whut?* blog post.

"You're kidding me with this."

"Read it! Read it. Read it read it read it. Read it. Nick. Nick. Nicknicknicknicknick read it read it read it. READ IT."

"So you're saying you want me to read this?"

"Nick! Read it! He knows. HE KNOWS WHAT'S GOING ON AT AUXANO."

Nick hunched over to read the article. Jay was right—The Hammer was alarmingly not totally wrong. It was bizarre that eight kids from the same small town had made the highest test scores in the state, and it wasn't a coincidence that all of those kids had parents who worked at Auxano.

But still. Everyone (except Jay) knew that The Hammer was a total kook. "It's interesting," Nick admitted.

"It gives me an idea," Jay said.

"Of course it does."

"Let's find The Hammer and tell him our story!"

"What story?" Jilly asked, waddling in from the kitchen with a large bowl of watermelon chunks.

"Vittles!" Jay cried, bouncing up and trying to pluck a piece of watermelon from the bowl. Jilly turned to him and let out an alarming snarl. Jay recoiled.

"Don't touch a pregnant lady's snacks," Molly called from the kitchen.

"All of that is for you?" Jay asked.

Jilly let out an audible growl.

"NEVER QUESTION A PREGNANT LADY'S SNACKS!" Molly yelled.

Jilly plopped down on the sofa and began to pop watermelon chunks into her mouth. "What story are you talking about?" she asked, eyeing the computer. "Is that my laptop?"

"Sorry, Jilly," Nick said, picking up the laptop to hand it to his aunt, and then setting it back down on the coffee table as she made it clear with hand gestures that watermelon holding and eating took precedent over laptop retrieval. "Jay was just reading an article about all the kids at school who aced the exam."

"Didn't you ace the exam, Jay?" Nick's mom asked, coming down the stairs into Molly and Jilly's living room. She was still looking a little worse for wear after her stay in the hospital for smoke inhalation, and Nick was trying, and failing, to not look worried every time he saw her.

"I did, I did," Jay said, his brow furrowed.

"That's wonderful," Nick's mom said, settling in on the sofa next to her son and gently tugging the hair on the back of his head, which was Mom-language for *You need a haircut*. Normally Nick would react by hunching his shoulders and pulling away (because he hated getting haircuts—it was fifteen agonizing minutes of torturous boredom and being forced to stare at himself in a mirror), but he didn't move. It was just his mom's way of telling him that she loved him. And he probably needed a haircut.

"Is it, though?" Jay muttered, staring at the laptop.

"Of course it's wonderful," Nick's mom said, rolling her eyes a little. "Your parents must be proud. I should call your mom to congratulate her on having such a smart kid."

"Oh, she knows," Jay said. "But how much does she know?"

"Is Jay not making sense?" Jilly looked up from her half-eaten bowl of watermelon to ask. "Are the not-pregnant people in the room understanding what he's saying?"

"Never," Nick said.

Jay shot him a look. "Isn't it time for us to do that thing?"

"What thing?"

"The thing where boys run off to talk about private weird teenage-boy things," Jilly chimed in.

Nick looked at his mother. "Go, go," she said, dismissing him with a wave of her hand. "Stop looking at me like I'm in danger of collapsing and go."

Jay had already grabbed four clementines from the bowl on the kitchen counter and was heading out the door. Nick followed him and they walked down the street in unchar-acteristic silence for a few minutes before Jay veered off into the woods. The last time Nick was in those woods he'd had an altercation with some of the Farm Kids, only getting out of it unscathed because Ed the Invisible Bus Driver had pelted them with clumps of dirt. And now Ed was . . . no one knew where Ed was. They'd just left him in the Auxano labs to be dissected by mad scientists.

Jay grabbed Nick's hand. "Focus, man," he said, "you're shifting again."

"Maybe we shouldn't be so close to all these trees," Nick said. "Maybe I should stick to open fields. Forever. So that I don't accidentally merge into a tree. Or a building. I could live in the desert or something."

Jay rolled his eyes. "Hush your absurd face, you were doing much better at controlling your business. Now the question is, can I?"

"No," Nick said, "you have never ever been able to control your business."

"Now, now, you old gristmill, now is not the time for sarcasm." Jay seemed genuinely worried, which was a very not-Jay way of being. Nick stifled the urge to wonder aloud why Jay was calling him a gristmill (or what a gristmill even was). There was never a good explanation anyway.

"So what's on your mind?" he asked. They were deep in the woods now. Jay looked around theatrically and leaned forlornly on a fallen tree. Despite his Jaylike dramatics, Nick could tell that his best friend was genuinely upset.

"All right. So what do we know about all the high scorers? What do they all have in common?" Jay asked.

"They all go to Deborah Read."

"Well, duh, my dear boy," Jay said. He began to pace. "What else?"

"They're all human beings."

"Again, your powers of observation never fail to astound. All of the high scorers—myself included—have parents who work for Auxano."

Nick thought a moment. "Okay, true, but half of the kids at school have at least one parent who works for Auxano. And if you've got a parent who works for Auxano it stands to reason that they make you study a lot so you can be smart like them. Like your parents," he added.

"Sure, sure," Jay said, rubbing his hands through his dark blond curls. "Clearly causation does not imply correlation."

"What?"

"Never mind." Jay stopped pacing and looked up at Nick, his face full of worry and doubt. "What if I'm not actually smart?"

"What do you mean?" Jay was the smartest kid in the school—everyone knew it, as sure as everyone knew that he was also the weirdest kid in the school (although Martina Saltis could probably give Jay a run for his money—she was just a quieter sort of weird). "Of course you're smart. About some stuff. Book stuff."

"Smart like Izaak Marcus?"

"What? Izaak Marcus is an idiot."

"Of course he is!" Jay nearly shouted. "I once saw him eat a whole jar of pickled eggs on a dare."

"I remember that! He barfed everywhere."

"Of course he did. Because he's very stupid. And yet here we are, me and Izaak, both sporting the highest scores on the exam, and both of us with parents who work at Auxano."

"Well, yeah, because he was given the formula. There's no way that he could have scored that high without it."

"And . . ." Jay paused. For the first time in their friendship Nick could see that Jay was thinking before he spoke. "And what if he wasn't the only one who was given the formula?"

"You think some of the other kids were given it as well?" Nick asked. "Sure. Claire Jones is definitely not that smart."

"What if we were all given the formula?"

"What do you mean?"

"I mean," Jay said, his voice quivering a little, "what if my parents gave me the formula? What if they've been using me as a lab rat?"

"What? No." Nick shook his head. "You've always been smart."

"Yes, yes," Jay murmured, still pacing, "yes, and also incredibly handsome, but let's be objective here. My parents are scientists. They work at Auxano. I have always been smart, which you could say was a trait I inherited from my brilliant parents. But, BUT, what if I didn't? What if I was just the first kid to get the formula?"

Nick blinked a few times. In all the years he'd known Jay—their whole entire lives—he'd never seen his friend have an inkling of self-doubt. Watching him question his own intelligence (something Nick did to himself all the time) was perhaps the most unnerving thing to have happened, and in the past few weeks Nick had been in a bus accident, gained the power to teleport, broken into a lab, and been assaulted by chemically weaponized screaming bunny rabbits. Jay's self-doubt was, incredibly, somehow worse.

"No," Nick said gently, "you know that the formula that

24

messed with the rest of us was only developed a little while ago. You've been at the top of the class forever."

"Sure. But is it completely beyond belief that my own parents could have been part of the whole project to enhance human potential from the start? Who is to say that they haven't been using me as guinea pig the whole time?"

"Jay . . ."

"What if I'm not who I think I am? What if I've been genetically engineered to be an incredibly handsome genius? And if that's the case, who would I have been otherwise?"

"Jay, stop." Nick stood up and put his hands on Jay's slight shoulders. "First of all, I don't think that your parents are some mad scientists who used their own son in their experiments. If they did, they'd probably pay more attention to you."

Jay thought a moment. "You know what, old saucer? You have a point. What's the second thing?"

"Second," Nick continued, "even if your parents did do something to you, there's no going back. You're still you."

Jay let out a sigh and then straightened up. "You know," he said with a bit of the old Jay Carpenter twinkle in his eye, "you're smarter than you look."

"I'm choosing to ignore that."

COOKIE WAS AS UNNERVED AS MARTINA WAS CALM AS they walked to the woods that connected the neighborhood to the school. "Did you hear me?" she asked, incredulous despite the fact that she had specifically aimed to get Martina's attention.

"Not with my ears."

"But . . . in your mind?" Cookie felt a chill run down her spine.

Martina looked at her with bright blue eyes. "Well, yes. Wasn't that your intention when you thought to me?"

"Yes, of course, I just didn't know if it would work." Cookie leaned against a tree.

"It worked."

"I can see that." Cookie thought a moment.

"Yes," Martina responded. "I can hear you now, too."

"What was I thinking?"

"Can you not remember? You just thought it."

"Martina!"

"You were telling me to let you know if I could hear you. And now you're annoyed with me."

Cookie gasped. "I didn't even mean for you to hear that!"

"I didn't, you just seem annoyed. Are you worried about people being able to hear what you're thinking?"

Cookie was. She nodded.

Martina went back to drawing in her sketchbook. "I

wouldn't worry about that. I don't think people can hear you unless you want to be heard." She looked up. "But try not to think anything terrible, just in case."

"Like what???"

"I don't know. Bad things. Murder. Stealing."

"Getting into a car that doesn't belong to us with an unlicensed underage driver and crashing it into a bunch of stuff?"

"Right. That sort of thing."

"HOW CAN I NOT BE THINKING ABOUT THAT SORT OF THING WHEN IT JUST HAPPENED?" Cookie exploded. "HOW CAN YOU BE SO CALM ABOUT ALL OF THIS?"

Martina smiled at Cookie. "Hey, I totally didn't hear you thinking that."

Cookie paused. "Really?"

"Really!" Martina said. "I just heard you yelling it. I think people can only hear your thoughts if you want them to. If you're giving directions, like when you wanted to meet me here, then people can get it. Just like you can hear when other people are thinking about directions." She put her sketchbook into her backpack and stood up. "Do you want to practice?"

Cookie looked at Martina. *Let's practice.*

For the next hour they worked on honing Cookie's new ability. Cookie would think something to Martina, and Martina would let her know if she'd heard her.

Pick up that rock would result in Martina picking up a rock and proudly presenting it to Cookie. *Clap your hands*, Cookie would think, and Martina would give her a short round of applause. Martina heard Cookie think *Climb that tree*, but refused. "I'm wearing a skirt," she explained.

"Okay, so you can hear me, but I can't control you."

Martina looked slightly disturbed. "Would you want to?"

"No!" Cookie said. "Well, I wouldn't want to control *you*."

"But maybe you'd want to control someone else?"

"I could command Jay to stop making gross comments about the future biracial babies he's convinced we're going to have," Cookie muttered.

"Why would you need to do that when you could just explain to him why that's not all right?" Martina asked.

Cookie looked at her. Martina Saltis had a way of making everything seem so much simpler and at the same time preposterously impossible.

You didn't just tell people how to act; they should already know. Was Cookie supposed to be responsible for how other people thought and behaved? If she had the power to make them not act like fools, maybe she would use it, but talking to someone was not a power. It was work, and as far as Cookie was concerned it was not her job to be the Friendly Brown Person in Muellersville who kindly educated everyone on what was and wasn't okay to say. People should care enough to figure it out for themselves.

Of course, Cookie knew that they wouldn't. Why would people change the way they acted if no one had any objections? But if Cookie could make them stop without having to say a word . . . now, that would be something.

She could make Jay stop giving his "compliments." She could force Sam Stoltzfus to never make monkey noises at her ever again. Or any noises! She could make sure that Emma Lee stayed away from Addison and Claire . . .

"Are you trying to think something at me right now?" Martina asked. "Because I'm not hearing anything."

"Nothing . . . I wasn't thinking any directions," Cookie said. "How far do you think my thoughts go?"

"You called me out of my house."

"But I was practically standing outside your window. Let's see how far we can go."

They spent another hour testing the limits of Cookie's range. Martina went a little ways down the footpath that ran through the woods, and then farther, and farther, until Cookie could no longer see her, and then farther still until she could hardly hear Martina yelling her own thoughts. She jogged through the woods to meet up with Martina and was surprised by how far the blue—brown—gray-eyed girl had gone.

"Wow," Cookie said. "We're almost at the school."

"Do you think you can think farther?"

Let's try.

FARSHAD NEEDED AIR. HE'D JUST SPOKEN WITH HIS uncle in Michigan and knew that if he had to talk to one more relative he was going to get rude. He put on his running clothes and told his mom that he was heading out.

"But I was just about to call Manoosh . . ." Farshad heard her say as he closed the door behind him.

I should go to the woods, he thought. Usually he liked running on even sidewalks, but it was as though the woods were calling to him, somehow. *And I should probably pick up some ice cream on the way. And spoons.*

What?

That was ridiculous. He wasn't about to go jogging with ice cream and spoons. And he wasn't even hungry.

I should get pistachio.

Farshad stopped, confused for a moment, and then concentrated on how to plunge a toilet before heading to the forest behind the school. Martina looked very pleased to see him; Cookie, not quite so much.

"Was that necessary?" she snapped at him.

"Did you use your powers to try to make me buy you ice cream?" Farshad snapped back.

"It was an experiment. I had to see if it worked."

"So I experimented back."

"Always with the toilets, though. What's wrong with you?" Cookie crossed her arms.

"Why are we talking about ice cream and toilets?" Martina asked.

"Yes, why are we talking about ice cream and toilets?" Jay and Nick came down the path, holding hands. It reminded Farshad of visiting Iran, where seeing men walking hand and hand down the street was no big deal; men there did it all the time. If you were friends with somebody, holding their hand was not weird. Farshad felt a rush of emotion that he couldn't quite define; a strange sort of longing. He looked at Martina, whose eyes turned a deep, alarming blue. She looked away from him to Cookie.

"Did you call them as well?"

Cookie looked confused. "No, I didn't. Or, at least, I didn't mean to. I wasn't thinking about them at all."

"Now, now," Jay said, bouncing up to Cookie with a gleam in his eye, "let's not pretend that you aren't thinking about me pretty much all the time. Now, why are we talking about ice cream and toilets?"

Farshad looked at Cookie. "She was able to call to me. With her thoughts."

Nick gaped. "Really?"

Martina nodded. "Really. We've been practicing."

"Do me! Do me!" Jay yelped.

Cookie rolled her eyes. "I'm not here to entertain you."

"Come on. Come on!" Jay hopped around excitedly. "Danie-sha, my steaming mug of sweet cocoa. Please. This is extraordinary. I need to know how this works. You're—"

Jay stopped. Farshad could easily tell that Cookie was angry, but Cookie being angry had never stopped Jay from talking before (in fact, in the very short amount of time that Farshad had been hanging out with Jay, he'd never seen him stop talking . . . ever). But here he was with his mouth still hanging open with unspoken words.

"Did you hear her?" Martina asked Jay.

"Yes," Jay whispered.

"Did she tell you to stop talking about her skin color?"

Jay looked at Martina. "Not in those exact words," he said quietly, and turned back to Cookie. "You know I'm only saying that stuff because I think you're beautiful, right?"

Cookie's eyes narrowed as she looked at Jay.

"Stop," he whispered.

Martina looked worried.

"Please, stop—" Jay implored. His eyes were filling with tears.

"Cookie," Farshad started. He wasn't clear on what she was projecting into Jay's brain, but whatever it was, it was hurting him.

"Daniesha . . ." Jay let go of Nick's hand and fell to his

knees on the forest floor, and for a moment all was silent. It seemed to Farshad that even the bugs and birds had stopped their chittering. A week or two ago he would have dismissed that as his own imagination, but after all he'd seen, anything was possible. "Cookie," Jay said with two fat tears rolling down his freckled cheeks. "Cookie, I'm sorry."

"Okay," Nick said firmly, stepping in between Cookie and Jay. "That's enough."

"It's okay," Jay said from behind him.

"It's not okay. We don't use our powers to hurt people."

"Since when?" Farshad asked.

"Since . . . since we're not supervillains?" Nick looked at Farshad. "I mean, we never had a meeting about it or anything, but I kind of assumed that it went without saying that we're not, you know, evil?"

"Maybe we should talk about it," Martina said.

"Wait, what?" Nick looked shocked. "What's there to talk about?"

Farshad took a step toward him. "What isn't there to talk about? This whole time we've just been running from one thing to another, trying to figure out what's happening to us, and in the meantime Cookie's powers are clearly getting stronger, and that's probably going to be happening to all of us." He looked at his thumbs. They seemed like normal thumbs, but ever since the accident Farshad had been hyper-aware of their power. He could use them to do whatever he wanted; he could use them to bust down doors and destroy cars and probably stop bullets (if the bullet hit one of his thumbs, which seemed unlikely, but still, he probably could stop a bullet if the shooter was an exceptionally excellent marksman and was aiming directly for them).

Farshad looked at the group. If Cookie was now able to project directions into people's minds, what would Nick be able to do? Teleport farther? Or maybe to the right? And what about Martina? The exact nature of her power wasn't really clear, but if she could change her eye color would she eventually be able to change other things about her appearance? Could she make herself look like a completely different person?

And what about him? What if the super strength spread to more than just his thumbs? Farshad imagined himself ripping one of the nearby trees out of the earth and hurling it. He could stop traffic, start avalanches—if the strength spread beyond his thumbs there's no telling what he might be able to accomplish.

"There are no rules for what is happening to us," he said.

"Well," Nick spluttered, blinking out of sight and reappearing four inches to the left, "there should be!" He rushed back over to where Jay was still on his knees and grabbed his hand. "Look what she did to Jay!"

"Really, Nick," Jay said quietly, "I'm fine."

Farshad looked over at Cookie, who had slumped against a tree. Whatever she'd done to Jay had clearly taken something out of her. "What did you do to him?" he asked her.

"Nothing," she whispered.

"Clearly you did something!" Nick blurted, helping Jay up. "Look at him!"

"Good sir," Jay said, "I am not an invalid."

"Whatever you did to him," Farshad said, taking a ginger step toward Cookie, "could you do it again?"

"Why?" Nick asked, getting more frustrated. "Why would she want to do"—he looked at Jay, who was looking a little shaky on his feet—"this?"

"It's not 'why would she hurt people,'" Martina said in her calm, slightly detached Martina way, "Farshad just wants to know if she *could*."

"Clearly she can!" Nick had his arm around Jay now, and Jay looked frail and small next to his much larger friend. "And she shouldn't!"

"But what if she needs to?" Farshad snapped. "What if any of us needs to use our powers to protect ourselves? We've done it before. I don't remember anyone having any objections to me using my thumbs to lock the Auxano goons in their own building."

"Plus," he continued, "the other kids who got the formula

are using it to gain an unfair academic advantage. What's to stop us from using our powers to get ahead?"

"There's 'getting ahead' and there's hurting people," Nick said angrily. "The kids who did well on the exam weren't hurting anyone. Cookie just hurt Jay. That had nothing to do with getting ahead."

"Don't be naïve," Farshad snarled. "By using the formula to 'get ahead' Izaak and his idiot friends hurt my chances to become valedictorian through hard work. Nobody is innocent here."

"Are you seriously trying to tell me that getting good grades is the same as . . . whatever she just did to Jay?" Nick looked aghast.

"You just don't understand because you've never tried to get good grades," Farshad snapped. "Some of us have worked really hard, and now it doesn't matter because all that hard work has been replaced with the good luck that some rich white kids had to have been born into families that are willing to give them experimental formulas to make them smart!" He found that he was shouting.

"So, what, we're supposed to be as bad as them?" Nick asked. "Just because they're cheating doesn't mean we have to turn our backs on basic human decency."

"That's pretty easy for you to say," Farshad said. "Have you ever been called 'Terror Boy'?"

"No . . ."

"He's been called fat," Martina chimed in.

"Hey," Nick said, hurt.

"Well, you have," Martina said matter-of-factly.

"Fine, but that doesn't give me the right to hurt anyone else," Nick said. "Why are we even talking about this? Why am I crazy to think that we should use our powers for good and not evil? Have you never read a comic book?"

He didn't understand. He couldn't understand, Farshad thought, what it was like to be the only Iranian-American in the school and to be tormented every single day because of where his parents were from and the foreignness of his name and the brownness of his skin. He didn't understand what it was like to have the one thing—ONE THING—that he did irrefutably better than anyone else taken away from him. Farshad had always had a plan—get good grades, get out of Muellersville, never come back—and now all that he'd worked for was basically meaningless because it could be bottled and sold in a formula. And now he wasn't supposed to use his superstrength in any way he pleased?

"Whatever," Farshad said, carefully putting his earbuds in and turning on the music. "I don't have time to be lectured." He jogged back down the path, out of the woods, and away from yet another thing in Muellersville that he could do without.

COOKIE WATCHED THE WHOLE EXCHANGE BETWEEN Farshad and Nick with a strange feeling of detachment, as if she were watching a television show. They were talking about her but no one was talking *to* her, a development that would have normally been irritating, but for once she was grateful to be part of the background.

And then she looked at Jay and she felt terrible. And also powerful.

She hadn't meant to hurt him. Or had she? It was difficult to tell. She had definitely wanted for him to shut up, true, and she wanted him to know what it felt like to be constantly reminded of how she wasn't like the other kids in Muellersville.

STOP IT, she'd thought at him in anger.

STOP IT RIGHT NOW, YOU'RE HURTING ME, she'd thought, and then she'd felt a surge of power as she watched Jay's eyes widen as her thoughts seeped into his brain. Cookie knew all too well exactly how unnerving it was to be forced into hearing the unwanted thoughts of others.

She should have stopped there, but making Jay Carpenter realize how gross his "compliments" on her skin and hair were was giving Cookie a feeling of intense power and control. She wanted to show him more, to let him know exactly how they made her feel. So she thought at him.

She thought at him about the time her mother took her to a playground when they'd first moved to Muellersville, and how she'd been playing with another girl and that girl's mother had snapped, "Get away from her! We don't talk to those people!"

She thought at him about the time that George introduced her and her mother to his own sister, and how she'd kept touching Cookie's hair and saying, "It's softer than I thought it would be!"

She thought at him about all the times one of the Farm Kids made monkey noises at her.

She thought at him about how Addison and Claire would always tell her how she was so lucky to be so unique and exotic.

She thought at him about how many times people were surprised that her mother worked at a prestigious place like Auxano.

And as she thought these things directly to Jay, more memories surfaced, until she felt like she was hurling her thoughts directly into his brain; every insult, every side-eye given by a shopkeeper, every time her intelligence was questioned—she put it all into Jay's head, and watched as the reality of her life as the only black girl in Deborah Read Middle School sank in. She kept hurling painful thought after painful thought, even after he'd asked her to stop, even after he dropped to his knees . . . If Nick hadn't stopped her, she might have kept going until Jay felt every last ounce of pain that his seemingly innocent little comments caused her.

Cookie was confused. Sure, Jay had it coming to him, but he was essentially a good person. Would he have stopped calling her things like his "Nubian princess" if she had just sat him down and explained why that was hurtful, like Martina had suggested? It was impossible to know.

Nick was agitated as they watched Farshad disappear down the path out of the woods. "Who does that guy think he is, anyway?" he fumed. "Should we be worried that he's going to do something stupid?"

"Probably not," Martina said. "He seems pretty smart."

"But also really angry."

"That's true," Martina said, thinking a moment. "He could do something stupid."

Nick threw up his hands in frustration. "You always know the least comforting thing to say."

"I have to go," Cookie said. She hadn't realized that she was going to say it, but now that it was said she turned on her heel and started walking out of the forest. Martina followed her.

"I don't want to talk about it," Cookie told her.

"Okay," Martina said, and they walked back in silence.

T HAD BEEN A HALF HOUR SINCE THE CHANCE-MEETING-gone-awry in the woods, and Jay still hadn't said a word to Nick. They'd walked out of the woods in silence, over the creek in silence, past the road that led out of town to the farmland in silence, and all the way to Jay's house in silence. Nick couldn't remember another time when Jay had been so quiet for so long, and that included ten days in the third grade when he'd had laryngitis and had insisted on communicating through a series of small percussion instruments (their teacher, Ms. Dean, put up with it for twenty minutes before confiscating Jay's collection of drumsticks, maracas, finger cymbals, and a little toy xylophone). Jay's silence was unnerving. Had Cookie damaged him? Permanently?

"Well . . . here we are," Nick said lamely outside of Jay's house, searching his friend's face for any sign of that old Jay sparkle. "Are you going to be all right?"

"Sure, sure," Jay said, distracted.

"Call me later?"

"Don't worry about me, old sod," Jay said, throwing back his narrow shoulders. "I merely have a lot of thinking to do."

"About what Cookie said? Er, thought?"

"Precisely. Precisely, old . . . I'm a little worn out, I'll think of a new name to call you tomorrow."

"Looking forward to it."

Nick headed back toward his aunts' place, thinking about what Cookie had done to Jay and the crazy argument he'd had with Farshad, and also that if he and his mom weren't able to move back into their own house soon he was going to have to drag his old bicycle out of the basement and find the pump to inflate the tires because Molly and Jilly lived too far from everything and this walking everywhere was getting old . . .

And then he was standing in the basement of his house. *What the . . .*

There it was, his old blue bicycle. It was covered in dust and the tires were definitely flat. Nick had no idea where the bike pump was, though. Plus, even if he did get the pump, and inflate the tires, his mom was going to ask all sorts of questions about how he had gotten into the house in the first place and GAAAAAAHHH HE HAD JUST TELE-PORTED OVER A BLOCK AND LANDED IN HIS OWN HOUSE. Nick felt dizzy and a little sick. He made his way up the stairs to the kitchen.

The house still smelled like smoke. Nick lurched to the sink and leaned over it to splash cold water on his face. He had done it. He had teleported farther than ever before, farther even than the day of the bus accident when he'd teleported himself out of the rolling bus and into the safety of the nearby field. But how? How had he done it?

"My room," Nick murmured to himself. "I command me to teleport me to my room!"

Nothing. He was still standing in front of the kitchen sink with water dripping off his nose. He grabbed a hand towel with a print of clocks on it and buried his face in it. He had to tell Jay about what had happened. Jay would be able to help him figure out how he'd done it. Jay would know where to start . . .

"GOOD GOD, OLD MAN!"

Nick looked up from the hand towel. He was in Jay's bedroom, with Jay sitting on his bed stark naked and staring at Nick with his mouth hanging open. Nick let out a shriek, took a step back, and tripped over a pile of books.

"WHY ARE YOU NAKED?" he bleated from his new vantage point on the floor.

"WHY ARE YOU HERE?" Jay yelped back.

"PUT ON SOME CLOTHING!"

"Nicholas! I. Am. In. The. Privacy. Of. My. Own. Room. I was doing some meditation, which was rudely interrupted by the likes of you."

"Jay?" Nick heard Jay's mother calling from downstairs. "Is everything all right?"

"Just fine, Mother!" Jay said.

"Is Nick there? I didn't hear him come in."

"That's because he teleported in, Mother!"

"Okay, just don't spend too much time on the Internet."

Nick reached for a pair of sweatpants that had been discarded on a pile of books and hurled them at Jay, who shimmied them on and then reached for a Rogue NASA T-shirt that was crumpled up on his bed. "You can look up now," he said when he was fully clothed. "I have covered my glorious body so you won't be blinded by its magnificence."

"Thanks for preserving my eyesight," Nick said wryly. It was a relief to hear the old Jay ridiculousness. "Sorry to interrupt your . . . whatever you were doing."

"I was meditating, you raw noodle. My experience with Daniesha earlier left me somewhat shaken and I wanted to clear my head."

"I didn't know that you meditated."

"I didn't know that you could teleport farther than four inches to the left. Apparently we do not know each other as well as we thought we did a mere five minutes ago."

"But since when do you meditate?"

"Since about ten minutes ago. It's very effective. Five more minutes and I might have reached enlightenment." Jay leapt off the bed and grabbed Nick by his shoulders. "Now let's talk about how on earth you just managed to beam into my room."

COOKIE WASN'T SURE HOW SHE AND MARTINA HAD ended up at the ice cream parlor, but there they were, sitting on the bench outside. Cookie had a cup of pistachio and Martina was sipping on a milkshake. Cookie took a bite of ice cream, and the cold sweetness of it helped to wake her up from the fog she'd been in since her confrontation with Jay.

"Does that help?" Martina asked.

Cookie took another bite. "I think so. Ice cream usually helps with most things." She sighed. "I don't know what I'm going to do."

"About what?" Martina asked, slurping her milkshake.

"What do you mean, about what? About my newfound ability to melt a dude's brain."

"Oh, that."

"Oh, that? OH, THAT?" Cookie stared at Martina, who seemed perfectly content to sit and sip her milkshake while Cookie grappled with issues of power and morality. "Doesn't it bother you that I can hurt people?"

"Sure it does," Martina said, "but you could always hurt people. Everyone can hurt people."

"Not everyone can melt a dude's brain."

"Sure they can. If they set the dude's head on fire."

"What do you mean?"

"I mean that everyone who is old enough to hold a bucket

of petrol and light a match can set a dude's head on fire. You throw the petrol onto the dude's head, then you light a match, and then you throw it at the dude. I mean, you'd have to be quick about it, but it is doable."

"That's horrifying!"

"So, whose head are we lighting on fire?"

Cookie looked up to see Addison, Claire, and Emma. Her friends. Well, Addison and Claire were her friends, anyway, or at least they had been up until their phones spontaneously broke. Addison looked surprised to see her with Martina. Claire looked angry.

"Don't bother telling me, I don't think I want to know," Addison continued. "Sooooo. What are you . . ." She looked at Martina, confused. ". . . ladies up to on this fine evening?"

"Nothing," Cookie said at the same time as Martina was saying, "Eating ice cream, I thought that was obvious." Cookie shot her a look. Was Martina trying to be weird in front of her friends? Probably not. Cookie had learned that Martina never tried to be weird, it just happened. *Don't be weird!* she thought desperately at Martina.

"I am a normal person," Martina said to Addison.

"Sure you are," Addison said warily. Martina slurped her milkshake.

"Hi, Cookie," Emma said. She was so annoying. Cookie did her best not to roll her eyes.

"Hey, Emma," she said.

"So, what have you been up to?"

"I know what she's been up to," Claire said. "She's been up to not caring at all that some of us did really well on the exams. She's been up to avoiding us. She's been up to hanging out with her new normal friend over here."

How. Dare. She. Cookie stood up and shoved her ice cream into Martina's hands (because she really couldn't be as intimidating as she needed to be if she was holding on to a cup of frozen deliciousness). "Oh really?" she asked quietly. Claire blanched. Cookie knew Claire had heard her use that tone of voice before and was terrified of it. "So what you're saying is that all your accomplishments basically mean nothing unless I congratulate you? Well, then. Congratulations, Claire. I would have thought all the banquets and newspaper articles would have been enough, but silly me, I forgot how important I am. So, good. For. You."

Claire sucked in a breath, and for a moment she looked like she was going to burst into tears. Addison burst out laughing. "Well, you know we can't live without you."

"I know, I know, I just forgot to put on my tiara this morning so I'm having an identity crisis," Cookie said, and turned back to Claire with a warm smile. "But seriously, Claire-Bear, congratulations. Your dad must be crazy proud."

"He is, he totally is!" Claire blurted, almost hysterical

with relief. Cookie smiled. Claire would always rather be on Cookie's good side, and getting too close to her . . . not-good side was terrifying enough to send her scampering back to the natural order of things, where Cookie was in control. "So . . . what are we doing?" She looked at Martina. "With our new friend?"

Cookie thought fast. *Just play along*. "This is Martina. She's awesome."

"Yes. I am. Very much so," Martina said, playing along.

Claire laughed nervously. "Cool."

"Yes. Cool," Martina agreed, and when Cookie looked at her she understood why Martina's older sister insisted on calling her "Martian." Martina didn't have actual antennae sticking out of her head but she moved through the world like she was a recent transplant from another planet who had read some books on human behavior without ever having any contact with an actual real-live human.

Addison eyed Martina. "So," she said, "are you going to Izaak's house tomorrow night?"

"I was thinking about it," Cookie said, trying to sound like she'd been invited.

"You should both definitely come!" Claire squeaked. "I mean, it's kind of a congrats celebration for the people who aced the test, but you should totally come anyway."

"Yes, that sounds like a cool thing to do," Martina said.

WHAT? SAY NO! TELL THEM THAT YOU'RE BUSY!

"Although we may also be busy with things that need to be done," Martina added.

NO, THAT YOU'RE BUSY. YOU. YOU ARE BUSY. NOT US. YOU.

"I am a particularly busy person." Martina smiled.

"Oh," Addison said, "but you should definitely come. It will be cool."

"Cool," said Martina.

"Cool!" yelped Claire, looking at Cookie.

"Cool," she said as noncommittally as possible. "Look, we gotta go now. See you later."

GO. GO. GO. SAY NOTHING ELSE.

Martina got up and waved a vigorous good-bye to Addison, Claire, and Emma as Cookie steered her away from the group. Once they were safely out of earshot Cookie scowled at the Martian.

"Why did you say that you wanted to go to the party?!"

"Because I was acting normal. Normal people like to go to parties, yes?"

"Well, yes . . ." Cookie said, exasperated.

"And if we go to a party with the kids who we think were treated with the formula by their parents we might get clues about what happened, right?"

Cookie hadn't thought of that. All she had been thinking

was how weird and awkward it would be to attend a social function with Martina. But the Martian had a point. "Sure," she said lamely, "but with all those thoughts swirling around I wasn't sure that I'd be able to control my power."

"No, you just thought I'd embarrass you in front of your old friends," Martina said, her eyes turning from a light blue to a rich brown as she looked at Cookie. Cookie started to protest, thought better of it, and stopped. Lying to Martina was useless. Not only did she know the truth, but she didn't seem to care.

"I'm sorry," Cookie said. "But I still don't know if it's a great idea."

"Oh, it's a terrible idea," Martina said, and resumed walking. "But we should still do it. Also, you're getting a lot better at directing your thoughts to me."

"I am?"

"Absolutely."

"Thanks, Martina. That actually makes me feel better."

"Okay."

"But, if we're going to do this, we have to take care of a few things first," Cookie said, heading off in the direction of her own house. "Come with me."

FARSHAD WAS STILL FUMING WHEN HE GOT HOME. HE had run for an hour, hoping to work off some of his anger, but it was still there. Nick's words were rattling around his brain as he got to the kitchen and poured himself a cup of water, ever mindful of his ability to accidentally shatter the glass with his indomitable thumbs. Constantly being aware of his thumbs was exhausting.

But in a way Farshad was used to it. Ever since he was little he'd always had to keep his strengths in check. Sure, he could get the best grades, but even before he'd become the school pariah, he'd known not to flaunt them. His parents had even sat him down and told him not to show off, ever, because no one liked a show-off. It was okay—great, even!—to crow about his accomplishments to his family, but not to other people. You know. Non-Persians.

So Farshad had learned to be humble. He'd ace a test but act like it was no big deal. He'd score the winning soccer goal but be the first to congratulate his teammates. He was just a normal American kid, nothing special, nothing to see here . . .

And for what? Why had he gone through all the effort to appear normal and likable when in the end they all turned on him anyway? Why was he trying to hide his crazy-powerful thumbs when he could use them—

The glass smashed in his hand. Farshad looked around

nervously to see if either of his parents had heard before gathering the shards of glass and throwing them out. He had to stop doing that. Or maybe just stop drinking out of glasses. Or stop thinking about what Nick had said.

Farshad recognized that Nick didn't have it easy. Everyone remembered when Nick's father had passed away—he'd been out of school for a while, and after the teachers sat them down and told them what had happened the kids would talk about it in hushed tones. There were plenty of kids in the school who had only one parent, but that was usually because of divorce or one parent had been called up for military service or something, not because they died. It was unthinkable, and that's why for a while most kids had given Nick a wide berth. They'd even left Jay alone (for a little bit) because they knew that he was Nick's best friend.

And Nick, to his credit, had never taken advantage of the sympathy or used it as an excuse to act out. He'd come back to school and kept his head down, and after some time people stopped talking about it and went back to stuffing Jay into lockers and flushing his head down the toilet. Most people probably forgot about it; Farshad certainly had until Mr. Friend had set Nick's house on fire and Nick and his mom had to move in with his aunts.

Farshad thought for a moment about Mr. Friend, and his and Abe's decision to leave him trapped in the secret lab at

Auxano. Would Nick have risked himself to get Mr. Friend out? Even though Mr. Friend had almost killed his mom? Probably, because Nick was soooooo good. Farshad felt himself getting angry again and forced himself to take a few deep breaths so he wouldn't accidentally smash something else.

He couldn't just be . . . good. The world as Farshad was coming to know it was not a good place. It was a world where completely undeserving kids got to advance well beyond their capabilities because their parents had gamed the system, and that had been happening even before they were all "Oh, and here's a magic potion that will make you not a huge idiot!"

It wasn't fair. And Farshad knew enough to know that life wasn't fair; it wasn't fair that Nick's dad had died, and it wasn't fair that Mr. Friend was trapped in some lab prison, and it wasn't fair that kids avoided Farshad just because his parents were from Iran. Farshad understood all of it. But why couldn't he at least try to make things a little more fair by taking advantage of his power the way that the Company Kids were taking advantage of theirs?

Farshad looked at his thumbs. What could he do with all that power?

What wouldn't he do?

Wait. Are you a Russian spy?
If I were I wouldn't tell you.
You know, I was joking, but now you're sort of freaking me out.
What do you think of this skirt?
It looks like a flower drank fruit punch and then threw up on it.
Perfect.
Now let's work on acting normal. Telling people that you're normal isn't going to cut it.

**ICK AND JAY HAD DECIDED TO RELOCATE TO** Nick's house (walking there this time instead of teleporting). "It occurs to me," Jay said, once they were out of earshot of Dr. Carpenter, "that your power is increasing."

"Funny, that occurred to me as well after I teleported into your room," Nick said.

"But it's not just you," Jay said. "Clearly Cookie is also getting stronger."

Nick looked at his friend as they walked, and could see that Jay was thinking before he spoke again, a rarity in Jay. "What exactly did she do to you?" he asked.

"Oh . . ." Jay said lightly, "this and that." Nick frowned at him and he let out a soft laugh. "Look, you old minotaur, I'm fine. Really. I just have to sort out some thoughts that she put into my head."

"What kinds of thoughts?"

"She made it clear to me that some of the things that I say can be insensitive. Things that I'd always thought were okay. Flattering, even. I never meant to hurt her. Or anyone! " Jay looked at Nick. "Nick, do I ever hurt your feelings with my words?"

"What, like when you just called me an old minotaur?"

"Did that injure you? I'm so sorry, Nick."

"No, no, it's fine, stop." Nick laughed. "I don't mind being called a mythical maze-dwelling beast."

"A MIGHTY mythical maze-dwelling beast. I really did mean it as a compliment." Jay looked worried.

"And that's fine. I don't care. But it's basically nonsense."

"GASP."

"Did you just say the word 'gasp' instead of actually gasping?"

"It's something I'm working on. I can't believe you called my beautiful words nonsensical."

Nick turned to Jay. "When you call me a minotaur I'm not going to care. When you point out, constantly, that Cookie is black by talking about her skin tone you're singling her out as being different." Jay started to say something but Nick kept talking. "Even if you mean it as a compliment. Don't you think that she knows she's the only black girl in the school? Do you think she needs you constantly reminding her?"

"She definitely made it clear that she doesn't," Jay admitted. "And now I'm wondering if everything that comes out of my mouth hurts people the way I hurt her. I felt it, Nick. She made me feel how much I'd hurt her." Jay stopped walking and looked stricken. "Maybe this is my superpower. I can hurt people with *my words*."

"Nah, most people don't pay that much attention to anything you say," Nick said.

"Owchies, Nicholas, you saucepan. That wounds."

"See? Anyone can hurt with their words." They'd reached Nick's house. The door was, unsurprisingly, still locked, so they headed into the backyard.

Jay looked around to see if any of the neighbors were around. The coast was clear. "Okay, try thinking about your bedroom. No, your kitchen, that's closer to the back door, so you can let me in. Think! Think with all your minotaur might."

Nick closed his eyes and pictured his kitchen. The table that his mother was always trying and failing to keep clear of bills and notices and old To-Do lists. The fridge with faded photos of Nick as a fat baby and toddler Jay dressed as a ladybug for Halloween. The ultrasound of Jilly's baby. The sink where he'd been not an hour before, splashing cold water onto his face. He opened his eyes.

He was still in the backyard standing next to Jay. "I don't think that worked."

"Interesting. Were you thinking of the kitchen?"

"Of course I was. I pictured the whole room in my mind."

"Same as the last time?" Jay asked.

"No, the last time I was thinking about being in my basement, and that's where I ended up."

"Why ever were you thinking about being in the basement?"

"I was thinking about how I wanted to use my old bicycle."

"AHA."

"Aha?"

"Yes, aha. It's not about the thinking," Jay said, jabbing Nick's forehead with his finger. "It's about the wanting." He poked the same finger at Nick's chest. "You weren't thinking about the basement. You were wanting your bicycle. And you weren't thinking about my room, you were wanting to talk to me."

"Gasp."

"Exactly. We just have to think of what you really want and—"

Jay had stopped talking. No, Jay may have still been talking, but Jay was no longer anywhere to be seen. Neither was Nick's backyard.

Nick felt the lump in his throat and he dropped to his knees in front of his father's gravestone. "Hi, Dad," he said softly. "I really need to talk with you."

So Claire tells me you're coming to our little soiree tomorrow.
Maybe. If you're lucky.
Oh, I'm lucky.
Why?
Excuse me?
Why are you lucky?
Uh...because I am. Is she coming with you?
Maybe. If you're lucky.
I don't know if I'm that lucky.
You're not.
We're leaving now.
Toodles!

TOODLES?" COOKIE ASKED MARTINA. "WHEN DURING our How to Be Normal tutorials did I ever utter the word *toodles*?"

Martina shrugged. "I like the sound of it. It rhymes with noodles."

Cookie sighed. "Come on, Toodles, let's get to class."

"I didn't mean for it to be my name . . ."

"Yeah, yeah."

They walked into Mrs. Whitaker's class and took seats next to Addison and Claire. Cookie could see Claire shooting Addison a look and didn't need her power to know what that look meant: *Why is Cookie hanging out with that weird girl all of a sudden?*

Whatever. They'd been through a major accident together; of course she was hanging out with Martina. Claire and Addison would just have to deal with it.

"It's cool that you guys are friends now, after the accident," Addison said to them, and looked confused. "I mean," she continued, "I guess you guys have been through a lot together."

Martina looked at Cookie, her gray eyes wide. *I didn't mean to put that thought in her head!* Cookie thought at her.

Be careful, Martina thought back.

Cookie smiled at Addison. "Yeah, and Martina's cool. She's a really good artist."

"Cool," Addison said.

"Cool!" Claire said.

"Yes," Martina said, "cool."

"Okay!" Mrs. Whitaker said, clapping her hands together once to silence the chattering class. "Are we missing anyone today?" She looked at her attendance book. "Where are Eric Mathes and Michael Donovan? And has anyone seen Nick Gross?"

Cookie looked around the classroom. Nick wasn't there. She looked at Martina, who gave an almost imperceptible nod—Eric Mathes and Michael Donovan were two of the Company Kids who had high test scores.

"Okay, guys, let's all pick partners and talk about DNA while looking at our fingers," Mrs. Whitaker said as she handed out worksheets. "Who has mid-digital hair?"

For the next five minutes Cookie and Martina worked together to answer the worksheet questions. Were they male or female? Did they have mid-digital hair? Were they able to curl their tongues? What color eyes did they have? (Martina answered "brown" just to be on the safe side.)

"Now we're going to pretend that each pair is going to have an offspring," Mrs. Whitaker told the class.

"Oh, Addison, we're going to make the most beautiful babies!" Claire joked, causing everyone to giggle.

Mrs. Whitaker rolled her eyes. "And we're going to see

if we can predict what sort of genetic traits the imaginary offspring will have . . . Well hello, Mr. Mathes, Mr. Donovan, how nice of you to finally join us. Do you have late passes?"

Eric and Michael swaggered into the room, completely ignoring Mrs. Whitaker and heading to the back of the lab where she kept the class hamster. Cookie had known them for as long as she'd been in Muellersville. Eric and Michael had never been very bright, but they weren't usually rude. Maybe to someone like Jay Carpenter, but not to one of their teachers.

"Boys," Mrs. Whitaker said in a stern voice, "if you don't have late passes you can't come in here. You know the rules."

Eric looked back at the teacher for a moment with a mean smile on his face before lifting up the hamster cage from the windowsill.

"Put that down this instant!" Mrs. Whitaker cried out, alarmed, as Michael let out a short, sharp bark of a laugh.

"I tell you what," Eric sneered, "I'll put down Neil deGrasse Hamster if you put down your little attendance book." He held out the cage. "Or we could just do some Galileo gravity tests." He let go of the cage and quickly caught it again. Someone in the class gasped. Michael laughed. Neil deGrasse Hamster let out a little rodent shriek.

"MR. MATHES!" Mrs. Whitaker roared.

Put the hamster cage down and GET OUT OF THIS CLASSROOM.

Eric put the cage down, and lurched back across the room to the door. "Dude," Michael asked, "where are you going?"

AND PINCH MICHAEL'S BUTT.

Eric's hand began to reach for Michael's pants. "Wait, what?" he muttered, snatching his hand away.

"Dude, what are you doing?"

"I don't . . ."

"BOTH OF YOU, OUT." Mrs. Whitaker shoved two disciplinary passes into their hands. "I expect better from kids who test so well. Maybe you can explain to Principal Jacobs why you think it's okay to come into my class late and threaten the life of Neil deGrasse Hamster. OUT."

Eric muttered something nasty and took a step toward Mrs. Whitaker.

OUT.

Eric and Michael left the room. "Back to your questionnaires," Mrs. Whitaker said, her voice a little shaky. She picked up the class phone to call the front office.

Martina picked up the hamster cage and put it back on the windowsill. She came back to the lab table and looked at Cookie with a raised eyebrow. Cookie smiled a little and shrugged.

She could get used to this.

ID YOU HEAR THAT ERIC ALMOST KILLED NEIL deGrasse Hamster?"

"Seriously?"

Farshad pretended to look for something in his locker while the two girls next to him continued their conversation. He'd gotten good at that over the years—making himself invisible, or as invisible as a really tall brown-skinned guy could be at Deborah Read Middle School. Ever since he got the name "Terror Boy" he had learned to deflect attention. The girls kept talking as if he weren't there.

"Eric's such a jerk," the first one went on. "He was just holding the hamster cage up like he was going to drop it and smash it if Mrs. Whitaker didn't, like, do his bidding."

"Like she was going to be all 'Sure, threaten the life of my pet and get what you want'? What is his problem?"

"I don't even know. All those high scorers are acting like they own the school."

"Gross."

"Super gross."

"Totally gross."

"It's so gross."

Maybe if Cookie were here she could use her powers to tell them to get to the point already. Farshad rolled his eyes.

"What's your problem?" the first girl asked. She was white with short curly hair and a freckled face.

Farshad felt his cheeks turning red. "Excuse me?" he stammered.

"Was our conversation not to your liking?"

"What . . . I . . ."

"Ugh, let's go," the freckled girl's blond friend said, dragging her away and giggling down the hall at what a freak he was. Farshad knew he'd be replaying the embarrassing scene over and over again in his mind for roughly the next fifty years.

"That looked very bad, young peppercorn." Jay Carpenter sidled up to him.

"That did not feel good," Farshad admitted, choosing not to ask why he'd just been referred to as a peppercorn. Or what a peppercorn even was. Nick always seemed to just ignore Jay when he was being bizarre, and Farshad was beginning to see the wisdom in that approach. He looked down at Jay, wondering for a moment if he'd recovered from his encounter with Cookie.

"What did you say to those lovely young women to make them turn on you in such a dramatic fashion?"

"It wasn't that dramatic," Farshad muttered.

"Certainly it was, you seem most put-out." Jay looked at the girls, and then to Eric Mathes and Mike Donovan, who were headed down the hall in their direction. "You know, I don't think those gentlemen went to the principal's office after all. Mrs. Whitaker is going to be apoplectic."

"Were you in the class with the hamster thing?" Farshad asked.

"Oh, yes," Jay said, "it was looking touch-and-go for Neil deGrasse Hamster for a moment there. But he's a stalwart rodent . . ." Jay's voice trailed off and they both watched as Eric and Mike hovered near Kaylee Schmitt, who was clutching her backpack. She did not look happy.

Kaylee was a Farm Kid. Farshad didn't know too much about her besides that; as a Farm Kid she had to get up extra early to take the small bus to school, she hung out with the other Farm Kids, and she did Farm Kid stuff (Farshad had no idea what that meant—he assumed it entailed lifting bales of hay, maybe? Milking cows? Whatever). Even though Farshad had never had any classes with Kaylee she was almost as tall as he was and hard to ignore. And now she looked trapped. "That doesn't look friendly," Farshad said.

"It most certainly does not," Jay agreed.

Mike leaned forward and said something to Kaylee in a low voice. She shoved him away and he grabbed her arm, and before Farshad could register what was happening Jay was bounding over to the tense trio.

"You have got to be kidding me," Farshad muttered to himself, and looked around for Nick. Nick was the only one who ever seemed to be able to control that little lunatic (well, and now Cookie, although she was nowhere to be seen, either).

"GOOD SIRS!" Jay yelped, inserting himself between Mike and Kaylee. "It appears that you are bothering this exquisite creature." He looked up at Kaylee, who appeared completely bewildered by his intrusion. "Do you mind if I call you an exquisite creature? I really do mean it as a compliment—" Mike's hand shot out and he grabbed Jay by the neck, slamming him into the row of lockers.

A small crowd gathered to watch Jay claw at Mike's hand around his neck. "STOP IT!" Kaylee screamed, punching Mike in the ear. He let go of Jay, who crumpled to the ground, and shoved Kaylee away. He raised his fist to hit her. "YOU BI—AAAAUUGH!"

Jay had bit him on the ankle. Farshad then heard the sickening sound of Mike's foot connecting with the smaller boy's stomach, and before he knew it he was running forward to save the valiant little biter. He grabbed Mike, pulled him away, and shoved him. Mike Donovan went flying fifteen feet down the hall, knocking over several other kids like bowling pins.

"TAKE THAT, YOU BRIGAND!" Jay yelped from his spot on the floor.

Farshad felt the wind getting knocked out of him as Eric tackled him. He managed to stay upright, but Eric had Farshad's arms pinned to his sides. Eric was *strong*. Farshad found himself having trouble getting oxygen to his lungs, and Eric slammed him into a wall. Farshad saw stars.

"GET OFFA HIM!" Kaylee jumped on Eric's back and wrapped her arms around his neck. Eric let go of Farshad, who stumbled backward. He tried to find a way to get to Eric without also hurting Kaylee, but she was riding the bully like an actual bucking bull.

It was pandemonium. Kids were screaming, Eric was lurching, Kaylee was holding on for dear life, and out of the corner of his eye Farshad could see Jay, still on the floor, looking for some way to bite Eric.

"THAT'S ENOUGH!" Farshad looked up to see Ms. Zelle making her way through the crowd. Eric threw Kaylee off his back and stared at the teacher, panting and heaving with a wild look in his eye. "Enough," Ms. Zelle said again. "You're coming with me. NOW. And you, too."

"But I didn't do nothing!" Kaylee yelled.

"Not you, him," Ms. Zelle said icily, looking at Mike, who lowered his head and came forward. "You. With me.

NOW." She grabbed both Company boys by the arms and led them away. The crowd began to disperse.

"Well, that was invigorating," Jay wheezed from his spot on the floor, not even bothering to try to get up.

Farshad bent over and put his head between his knees. "Everything hurts."

"*Pshaw*, you did great. Did you see how far Mike went?"

"That was crazy," Kaylee chimed in. "Thanks for helping me."

"All in a day's work, you glorious Amazon warrior," Jay told her. Farshad couldn't help but laugh. The little bug was starting to grow on him. "And how about my stupendous friend? You are truly a Sultan of Strength. Wait. Was that offensive?"

"Kind of, yes."

"I have so much to learn."

"You threw that jerk, like, really far," Kaylee pointed out. Farshad shrugged. "Well, thanks," Kaylee added quietly as she picked up her backpack and walked away.

"Very interesting," Jay said. "Very, very interesting."

"What, Kaylee?" Farshad asked.

"No, she's not that interesting. I mean, if you're into her I can see why. She is magnificent in battle," Jay said. "I'm saying it's interesting that Ms. Zelle was able to control Eric and Mike the way that she did."

"Huh," Farshad said. Jay was right. The Company Kids had seemed so unhinged until Ms. Zelle's arrival.

"Also," Jay went on, "it's pretty interesting that she took them in the opposite direction of the principal's office."

Farshad looked down the hallway where Ms. Zelle had taken Eric and Mike.

"Right toward the teachers' parking lot," he murmured. "Where's Nick?"

**ICK HADN'T ASKED HIS MOM IF HE COULD SKIP** school—he just didn't go. As far as he was concerned he'd earned the right to take a day off without having to pretend that he was sick.

He'd spent about fifteen minutes at his father's grave. He wasn't quite sure what he was supposed to do there. Talking seemed silly, because he knew that his dad was dead and couldn't hear him, and on the off-chance that his dad was somehow watching over Nick then he already knew everything that was going on so there was no need to go over it, right? When his father was in the hospital and he knew that he was dying he'd never said anything like "I will be with you and watching over you always, so feel free to come to me with your problems."

No, he'd just said, "Your mom knows me better than anyone else in the world, so if you ever need to talk to me, you can talk to her and she'll know what to do, okay?"

He probably hadn't predicted that Nick would have questions about what to do with the sudden ability to teleport. Because Nick was pretty sure his mother didn't have a clue as to what his father would have thought of this particular scenario.

Instead of talking, Nick spent the time cleaning up his dad's grave. It was pretty clean to begin with, but he cleared away some dead leaves and pulled a few dandelions out by the base of the gravestone. Once it was clean he headed back to his aunts' place, where Jilly was complaining loudly about false labor pains (seemed real to Nick, but what did he know) and everyone was too preoccupied debating what to do about that to pay attention to Nick. He sent a quick email to Jay to let him know that he hadn't completely vanished from existence and then went to bed without dinner.

The next day he set off as if to go to school but found his feet walking away from the campus. Down the sidewalks, over the footbridge, out to the cow path that twisted through the fields that surrounded Muellersville. He used to ride his bicycle down the cow path with his dad.

Don't think about the bicycle, he told himself, *you'll just end up back in the basement. And don't think about Dad, because there's nothing left at the gravesite to clean up.*

So what was he supposed to think about? Maybe Jay was onto something with the whole meditation thing. If Nick could clear his mind, he wouldn't worry about accidentally teleporting somewhere, or start freaking out about what would happen if his power continued to grow, like Willis, the kid they'd saved from Auxano . . .

And there he was, back in Beanie and Rebecca's apartment. Willis was sitting in a corner on the floor with his back to the room, surrounded by papers covered in haphazardly scribbled mathematic equations. Señor Fuzzybutt was on the floor, licking his . . . fuzzybutt. Rebecca was coming out of the kitchen, holding a plate of chicken nuggets.

"Mein gott!" she shrieked at the sight of Nick's sudden appearance, and the plate of nuggets clattered to the floor. Willis had no reaction. Beanie rushed into the room and stopped short upon seeing Nick.

"Uh . . . hi," Nick said after a tense moment. "I was just thinking about you guys, so . . . I'm here."

Rebecca and Beanie shared a look. "Did anyone see you come in?" Rebecca asked.

"Oh, I'm pretty sure that didn't happen," Nick said.

"Come, come, sit down," Beanie said, casting a worried look to Willis, who continued to scribble on his papers as if nothing had happened. Nick sat down on the sofa. Rebecca and Beanie looked at him. He cleared his throat.

"I think our powers are increasing," Nick said, and told them about how he'd come to suddenly appear in their apartment. "I can't seem to control it," he said. "I'll be thinking about a person or a place and all of a sudden I'm there."

Rebecca nodded as if she understood. Beanie nodded, too. Willis grunted, although it wasn't clear if that was in response to Nick's story or just a general sort of grunt.

"How . . . how is he doing?" Nick asked, casting a sidelong glance at Willis.

Rebecca sighed. "He's the same."

"Does any of . . . this"—Nick gestured to the papers that littered the floor—"make any sense to you?"

"Not at all," Beanie said with a sigh, "but if we don't give him more paper he just starts to write on the wall." He pointed to a spot in the corner where several mathematical equations had been hastily scribbled. "Do you know anyone who might be able to figure it out?" he asked, gathering some of the papers and handing them to Nick.

The fact was that because Auxano was such a major part of Muellersville there probably were some math geniuses that Nick knew—Jay's parents, for one. But even though Nick had assured Jay that they probably weren't involved in the development of a formula to make kids better testers, he wasn't totally certain. Maybe Farshad's parents would understand? That is, if Farshad would even talk to him—

"WHAT THE HELL, MAN!" Farshad yelped. Nick found himself in the school bathroom directly between Farshad and Jay, who were both using urinals.

"Well hello, you old toilet intruder, good that you could finally make it," Jay said, continuing to pee while Farshad scrambled to look presentable. "Now tell us, were you thinking about me or about this bathroom in particular?"

Nick quickly reached out to grab Jay's shoulder, thought

better of it, and grabbed Farshad's arm to keep from teleporting again. His other hand was still holding on to Willis's papers. "I was thinking of you," he told Farshad, who was staring at him, wide-eyed but not moving away. "Do you think your parents would understand any of this?" He looked at the papers.

"Let me see, let me see," Jay said, snatching the papers and peering at the equations. "Hmm. Interesting."

"Can you understand them?" Nick asked, surprised.

"Not at all, it looks like crazy-person nonsense. Where did you get these?"

Nick explained his morning to Farshad and Jay, who listened without interruption.

"Astounding," Jay breathed when Nick had finished.

"I'm not totally sure why you needed to include the detail about the cat," Farshad grumbled.

Jay looked at his watch. "Gentlemen, sixth period is about to let out. We should relocate before this bathroom is teeming with young men needing to relieve their bursting bladders."

"Wait, were you two cutting class?" Nick asked, suddenly aware of the oddness that was Jay hanging out with Farshad.

"You're not the only one who's had adventures, my dear left sock," Jay said. "To the Understeps!"

COOKIE HAD HEARD A LOT OF WILD RUMORS OVER the years (and had started quite a few of them), but it seemed like absolutely everyone was talking about how Eric and Michael had gotten into a fight with Kaylee Schmitt, The Shrimp, and Terror Boy.

"I totally saw it," Bethany Marino was telling anyone who would listen. "Terror Boy threw Mike Donovan across the hall, like, fifty feet or something."

"Wait, I thought I saw The Shrimp bite him," Nora Weir said.

"The Shrimp bit Terror Boy?" Claire asked.

"No, The Shrimp bit Mike. Before Terror Boy attacked him."

"So, wait, are The Shrimp and Terror Boy, like, friends now?" Addison asked, giggling.

"Yes," Martina said.

"Wait, what?" Claire asked. "How do you even know this?"

"Because they're my friends, too," Martina said. "And it's mean that you call them Shrimp and Terror Boy. Those aren't their names."

Claire stared at Martina. Addison gave Cookie a look. Cookie quickly turned to Bethany and Nora, who were clearly very excited to be the center of attention. "So why were they fighting?"

"I think Kaylee started it," Bethany said in a low voice. "You know how those Farm Kids are." The group nodded. Everyone did know how those Farm Kids were: big, dumb, and usually in trouble.

"How are Farm Kids?" Martina asked.

SERIOUSLY, STOP TALKING, Cookie screamed at Martina in her mind.

"What?" Martina asked. "I don't understand."

Cookie forced herself to laugh. "She's so funny," she said, suddenly incredibly grateful for the ringing of the seventh-period bell. This school day could not end soon enough.

We're at the Understeps. Cookie heard Farshad's voice in her head and immediately became annoyed. *Come to the Understeps.*

And then a moment later, *Please come to the Understeps.*

"Gotta go," Cookie said, grabbing Martina's arm and steering her away from Bethany and Nora, who were describing Kaylee's ugly outfit to Addison and Claire in great detail.

"Farshad wants to meet up with us," she whispered to Martina as they ducked around a corner to avoid being caught without a hall pass by Principal Jacobs. They quietly made their way to the Understeps, where Jay was lifting up his shirt and Farshad and Nick were inspecting his bare chest.

"Did we really need to be here for this?" Cookie asked, irritated, until she saw what were the beginnings of a massive bruise forming just below Jay's rib cage. He saw her looking and lowered his shirt.

"It's just a bruise," he said. "I am mostly intact."

"Did Mike Donovan do that to you?" Martina asked.

"He kicked Jay in the stomach," Farshad told her.

"Did you kill him?" Martina asked.

"No!"

"He did throw Mike down the hall," Jay said with pride. "It was magnificent. I doubt they'll be messing with us again."

"What are you talking about?" Farshad snapped. "Eric immediately tried to kill me."

"Except for that," Jay admitted.

"What did you do to make them come after you in the first place?" Cookie asked, before quickly reconsidering. "Oh, wait, never mind, you were probably just being you."

"In fact, I was," Jay said. "I saw a damsel in distress and I swooped in to save the day, as is my wont. The brutes were harassing Miss Kaylee Schmitt and I simply couldn't stand for it."

"Then why did they come after Farshad?" Martina

asked, looking at Farshad, who quickly looked down in embarrassment.

"Because he is my brother-in-arms!" Jay declared, clapping Farshad on the back before wincing in pain from the effort. "He rushed forward to aid me in battle, and for this I shall forevermore be indebted."

"So," Nick said carefully to Farshad, "you used your power for good, after all."

"Of course he did, he's my brother-in-arms," Jay scoffed, and Cookie had a sudden understanding that half of the goofy nonsense that Jay spewed was carefully calculated to deflect attention away from an embarrassed person. It was sort of brilliant.

(The other half of the goofy nonsense that Jay spewed was still pure goofy nonsense.)

"Mike and Eric were acting very weird in class," Cookie interjected. "Did you hear about how they threatened to kill Neil deGrasse Hamster?"

"Cookie saved him by using her power to tell Eric to put down the hamster cage," Martina added. "Her power is getting stronger."

"So is mine," Nick said in a low voice, holding out a handful of papers that were covered in what looked like mathematical equations. "Willis made these. I just teleported from Rebecca and Beanie's apartment with them."

Cookie stared at Nick, who was resting his hand on Jay's narrow shoulder. "Can you control where you go?" she asked. Nick shook his head.

"It's okay," Martina said, "I don't think Eric Mathes and Michael Donovan can control their powers, either."

"What do you mean?" Farshad asked.

"I mean, they're not the nicest boys, but they've never tried to kill a hamster before. Or tried to beat up three people in the middle of the hall."

Martina was right. As long as Cookie had known Eric and Mike they'd always been just . . . there, usually hanging out with Izaak. The worst thing they'd ever done was to give some nerds swirlies, but as far as she knew they'd never hit anyone hard enough to make a nasty bruise like the one they'd given Jay.

Cookie looked at Farshad. "Do you think they're stronger? Like you?"

Farshad thought a moment. "Eric was strong, but I don't think he's as strong as . . . my thumbs. He's a different kind of strong."

"What do you mean?" Nick asked.

"He's the sort of strong that you get when you don't care at all about what happens to the other guy."

"My brother Farshad is right," Jay said, making a move to clap Farshad on the back again and then thinking better of it (or he was just being restrained by Nick, who was still holding on to his shoulder). "I truly believe that Michael did not care about my well-being in the slightest when he rammed his foot into my solar plexus."

"Since when do guys care about how much they hurt each other in a fight?" Cookie asked.

"Well, no one wants to kill anyone else," Nick said. "Guys just want to show each other who is stronger without committing murder or looking like a psycho or getting suspended from school."

"All of that could be accomplished without fighting at all," Martina noted. She was sitting on the floor with her sketchbook out, again, and Cookie could see her sketching out the fight as if she had been there.

"Of course it could, but the males of the species have male hormones and that makes them do very stupid things," Jay said dismissively. "But do we think that these particular hormonal males are acting out more because of exposure to the Auxano formulas that they may or may not have been exposed to by their overachieving parents?"

Martina looked up. "Cookie and I can find out at the party tomorrow night."

"Party?" Jay perked up.

"It's a party for the high test scorers at Izaak Marcus's house," Cookie explained.

"Huh." Farshad glowered. "My invitation must have been lost in the mail."

"I don't think there were paper invitations," Martina said. "You probably weren't invited because Izaak doesn't like you."

"I think you're onto something there." Farshad took Willis's papers out of Nick's hand and stuck them in his backpack. "I have to go to class. I'll take these home and come up with some sort of excuse to show them to my parents to see if they mean anything or if they're just crazy-person garbage. You guys enjoy your party."

"Oh, I don't think we will," Cookie said weakly as he sauntered off. She turned to look at Nick only to find him gone.

"Oh dear, it's happened again," Jay said, looking worried.

"Where did he go?"

"I haven't the faintest idea." Jay looked up at Cookie. "Listen . . ."

"It's okay," she said.

"I just wanted to say . . ."

"Please, don't. It's fine. We're cool."

"Well and good, then," Jay said. He let out a sigh and winced again. "Now if anyone would care to accompany me, I'm not too manly to admit that I might need Nurse Biggs to take a look-see to make sure I don't have any broken ribs."

"You don't," Martina said, putting her sketchbook into her bag and standing up. "But you should put some ice on it."

"Thank you, Dr. Saltis."

"Wait," Cookie said. "How do you know?"

"I just do."

Cookie looked at Martina. Farshad was getting stronger. Nick was teleporting farther. Her own talent for reading thought directions was becoming an ability to give thought directions. But as far as Cookie could see, Martina was the same; just a normal, weird girl with randomly changing eye color. Or was there something more?

FARSHAD'S MOTHER HAD MADE *KHORAKE GOOSHT* for dinner, which usually put everyone in a good mood; Farshad's father liked to tell people that he married his wife for her brains but stayed for her cooking. Farshad had heard that joke repeated to nearly every dinner guest they'd ever had. He liked his mother's cooking just fine, although he secretly looked forward to the times when she'd be away at a conference, because that meant his dad would make macaroni and cheese from a box and put chunks of fried hot dogs in it. Farshad understood intellectually that his father's cooking was completely gross, but it was also really tasty. He suspected this was why his mother chose not to attend too many conferences.

"So," Farshad's mother said as she ladled the Persian beef stew over a bed of steaming basmati rice, "anything new at school?"

Keep calm, and act like everything that you're saying is totally true, because of course it is. "Actually, someone gave me some impossible math work as a joke."

"Ha! That's a good joke," Farshad's father said, shaking his head and smiling.

"Yes . . . it's hilarious. But I was thinking, wouldn't it be funny if you could actually help me to figure it out? It isn't for an assignment or anything, just for a laugh."

"I never understand what American teenagers find funny," Farshad's mother said.

"What are you talking about?" his father said. "It's very funny. We can go over it after dinner."

"Thanks, Baba."

"Of course, this is why I went and got those advanced degrees. So we can turn the tables on math jokesters." Farshad's dad rubbed his hands together gleefully as his mom shook her head in mock irritation.

When dinner was over Farshad handed the papers to his father with as much nonchalance as he could muster (sure, here's some crazy stuff written by an Amish teenager who is definitely not playing with a full deck of cards, no big deal) and then went to help his mother clear the table.

He was looking for dishwashing soap when he realized that his mother had abandoned him to finish the cleaning by himself. Farshad poked his head into the living room and saw his parents sitting next to each other on the sofa. Willis's papers were spread over the coffee table in front of them, and they were murmuring to each other in Farsi. Farshad's father was absentmindedly tugging at his beard and his mother was twisting her rings, things they usually only did when they were agitated. And they were definitely agitated.

"Farshad," his father said, looking up at him and speaking in a low voice, "where did you get these?"

"Oh, you know," Farshad said lightly, "like I said, a friend at school gave them to me. As a joke."

Farshad's parents looked at each other, and then back at him.

"Which friend, Farshad?" his mother asked quietly.

"Why, what's wrong with it?" he asked, trying to avoid having to name anyone. Something about those equations had definitely disturbed his parents and Farshad was suddenly filled with visions of them asking more questions than he cared to answer. He felt his thumbs twitch.

"Nothing," his mother said quickly, which was clearly a lie, as something was definitely wrong with the equations. "It's just that this is very advanced math, Farshad. Highly advanced."

"Oh, so you can't understand it? That's fine, you don't need to bother, it's a dumb joke anyway," Farshad said, forcing a chuckle.

"This is . . . sensitive information," his father said. "And we'd like to know where you got it."

"What do you mean?" Farshad asked.

"These equations," his mother said with hesitation, "these equations look very similar to some things that we've been working on at Auxano."

"Really?" Farshad said. "How weird."

"What's weird," Dr. Rajavi said, shooting a quick look to his wife, "is that these equations are done."

"Done?" Farshad asked with a strange feeling in his gut.

"Finished," Dr. Rajavi said, looking at the papers in her hands, which were shaking ever so slightly. "We've been working on these for a very, very long time without finding an answer. But this . . . this has the answers."

"Farshad," his father said in a low, almost frightened voice, "where did you get these? Who gave them to you?"

Farshad blinked. "Jay Carpenter," he said.

**W**ELL . . . IT WILL HAVE TO DO," COOKIE SAID, looking over her work. Martina looked nearly exactly like Martina always looked, only now she was wearing fake glasses that Cookie had found in a costume store. No one outside of their weird little group had seemed to notice her changing irises, but that was because no one ever paid much attention to Martina, and Cookie knew that was going to change now that Martina was hanging out with her. She was hoping the glasses would make the color changes a little less obvious.

"Do I look smarter?" Martina asked.

"Probably," Cookie said. "People with glasses always look smarter."

"That's strange," Martina noted. "I usually find that people with glasses just have poorer vision."

"Well, stereotypes suck," Cookie agreed, looking at her phone. It was almost time to go if they wanted to get there on time, which Cookie did not. Getting places on time was for people who did the waiting for people like her.

You have to find Jay. Farshad's voice was suddenly echoing in Cookie's mind as if he were standing right next to her. Or sitting inside of her brain. She froze.

What? No! RUDE. Get out of my brain.

"Cookie?" Martina asked.

Cookie, listen to me. You have to find Jay and tell him to meet us somewhere. Anywhere. But he has to get out of his house.

"Is it Farshad?" Martina asked.

What is wrong with you? Cookie thought, trying to get her brain to scream so that Farshad, wherever he was, would feel as uncomfortable as she was feeling with his voice in her head. *Haven't you ever heard of a phone?*

I broke my phone. With my thumbs.

"Ugh," Cookie said. *Frigging use your computer to message me.*

I kind of broke that, too.

Seriously?

Look, just call or text or think to Jay that he needs to get out of his house right now before his parents see him.

Why?

I'll tell you when I see you. Meet me at the spot in the woods.

I can't. Martina and I are going to the party at Izaak's house.

This is more important. Just come, and tell Jay to come.

STOP TELLING ME WHAT TO DO. I AM NOT YOUR MESSAGING SERVICE.

Okay! I'm sorry. Please. Please find Jay. Please.

FINE.

This is hurting my head.

No kidding.

Then silence. "He has got to stop doing that," Cookie growled. Martina looked at her. "Well, he broke his phone. And his computer. Anyway, he really wants us to find Jay before his parents do."

"Why?"

"I don't know, we both wanted to stop thinking to each other, so we'll find out when we see him in the spot in the woods." Cookie rubbed her temples. "I don't suppose Jay has a cell phone?"

Martina shrugged. "If he did I wouldn't know the number. Can you think to him?"

Cookie bit her lip. The idea of projecting any more thoughts into Jay's brain was more upsetting than she would admit to Martina. She had really hurt him, and as obnoxious as Jay could be, she didn't want to do it again. Cookie closed her eyes, and felt Martina's hand resting on top of hers.

"You'll be fine," Martina said. "Just stay calm."

"Okay," Cookie said.

Jay.

Jay, Farshad wants you to get out of your house right now. Leave before your parents come home, and meet us in the spot in the woods.

Cookie opened her eyes and let out a breath.

"He heard you?" Martina asked.

"I think so," Cookie said, grabbing her purse. "I got out of there pretty fast."

Martina nodded. "I think he heard you."

**ICK TOOK THE MUG OF HOT COFFEE FROM ABE OUT** of politeness and sat down at the Amish teenager's family kitchen. It was pretty sparse, as kitchens went: a small wooden table and chairs, a wood-burning stove, and what looked like an old-fashioned icebox. Nick had heard that the Amish didn't use electricity, but he hadn't expected everything to be so quiet.

No noise coming from a humming fridge, no lights coming from digital displays—Nick could think of at least three digital clocks in his aunts' kitchen (one on the microwave, one on the stove, another on the radio, and they were never in sync), and it was strange to not see anything. There wasn't even a wall clock.

Abe seemed agitated, which made sense, as he'd just witnessed Nick appear out of thin air. Nick had tried to calm him down by explaining how his own powers had expanded, but then he'd mentioned how he couldn't control them and Abe seemed ready for him to disappear at any second. Nick couldn't blame him. He half expected *himself* to disappear at any second. He took a sip of the coffee, and found that Abe had put so much sugar and heavy cream in it that it tasted like coffee ice cream.

"I keep wondering why you are suddenly here," Abe said, sitting down across from Nick with his own full mug.

"I'm telling you, I can't control it," Nick explained.

"Yah I know, but when you thought of the bike, you were in the basement, and then you thought of your strange little friend, and you were with him. So, were you thinking of me?" Abe looked at Nick.

"I don't know," Nick admitted. "Maybe? I've been thinking about everything. I can't stop thinking about everything that's happened since the bus accident. Can you?"

"No, for certain I cannot," Abe said. "But when I think about things I do not go flying around from place to place. It is a shame you cannot take people with you when you go."

"I don't know," Nick said, "before I couldn't go farther than four inches, and now I'm showing up all over the county. Maybe in a little while I'll be able to take other people."

"Perhaps you should practice," Abe said. Nick looked worried. "Let's go to the neighbor's barn and get a chicken for you to practice with."

"A chicken?"

"Yah, sure."

"Wait, I don't feel right about stealing a chicken."

"You will not steal! The chickens are ours. The neighbor is just holding them until we get a new barn that has not been burned down by a madman with fire-starting powers. Come."

"You look like you have never held a chicken before,"

Abe noted a few minutes later as Nick and the chicken Abe had shoved into his hands engaged in a tense staring contest.

"You are correct, I have not," Nick admitted. "What's this one's name?"

"She does not have a name. She is a chicken."

"Well, did you ask?" Nick said, nervous that the nameless chicken was going to start flapping and possibly pecking at his eyes. He was suddenly grateful for the poor eyesight that required him to wear glasses. "You can talk to animals. Ask her what her name is."

Abe sighed. "Fine." He looked at the chicken. "She thinks that's a stupid question."

"Really?"

"No, she is a chicken, she is thinking, 'Put me down.' But do not. Let's see if we can make you disappear with the chicken. Maybe think about a place you would like to be?"

Okay. Okay okay okay you can do this. Nick squeezed his eyes shut and thought about being back in the Zook family kitchen. He thought about the wood-burning stove and the mug that was still mostly full of sweet coffee, and the wooden table and the icebox. He gingerly opened one eye to find that he was still standing in a strange barn holding on to a nameless chicken.

"I didn't go anywhere."

"No, you are still here, holding a chicken."

"I'm going to name her. Maybe we'll have a successful journey together if we know each other a little better."

"Don't name her."

"Why not?"

"If you name her it will feel wrong to eat her."

"Rihanna! There. I've named her." Nick looked at Rihanna the chicken. "Now I've named you, so that dude can't eat you, and you owe me your life."

"Bok," Rihanna said.

"I do not think she likes her weird name. Perhaps she would rather be eaten," Abe said. "Try again."

For the next half hour Nick tried and failed to teleport

to Abe's kitchen while holding Rihanna. Then he gave the chicken back to Abe and tried to teleport to the kitchen without her for another half hour, to no avail, and it was starting to look like he was going to have to ask Abe and his deranged horse for another ride back into town.

"Maybe the problem isn't Rihanna," Abe wondered aloud. "Maybe you just don't want to go to my family's kitchen."

"I don't know about this," Nick said, flopping onto a bale of hay in frustration. "I've never been able to teleport with any other living thing before. In fact, touching a person or maybe a chicken is the only thing that keeps me grounded. It's probably better that I'm not able to bring anyone else with me."

"Bok," said Rihanna.

"See, Rihanna agrees with me."

"But what do you mean, you have never been able to teleport with anyone else before?" Abe said, irritated. "A few weeks ago you could not teleport at all. And then you could not teleport more than a few inches. Now you can go very far distances. You are getting more powerful, so it is not so crazy to think that you would be able to take someone with you."

"Well, it isn't happening tonight," Nick said. "Why are you pushing me?"

Abe threw up his hands. "Because, *dumkupp*, if you can

teleport with other people you can get people into places. And out of them."

Nick stared at Abe with a sudden understanding. "You want to break Mr. Friend out of Auxano."

"Of course I do!" Abe said, practically shouting (which for him still wasn't that loud). "Don't you? We just left him there!"

"So you want me to somehow teleport into Auxano, grab hold of a dude who blows stuff up with his mind and has no control over that, and then somehow teleport out of there without being blown up myself?" Nick asked, incredulous.

"We have to do something!" Abe said. "We just left him there!"

"Bok!" Rihanna said.

"What do you mean, we just left him there?" Nick asked.

"I mean that Farshad and I saw him at Auxano and did not know what to do, so we left him there. We said we would come back for him, but we were not able to."

Nick's head was spinning. "Why didn't you tell us this before?"

"Before, I didn't see a way to get him." Abe gave Nick a hard look. Sometimes he seemed much older than fifteen.

"Okay," Nick said, picking up Rihanna. "Let's keep trying."

"Bok," she said.

FARSHAD WAS ALREADY IN THE WOODS WHEN COOKIE and Martina arrived. "Is Jay with you?" he asked.

"Does he look like he's here?" Cookie snapped.

"No, no, I'm sorry," Farshad said, running his hands through his thick black hair. For a moment Cookie found herself wondering what his hair would feel like and then immediately felt weird about wondering such a thing. Whatever. He didn't have bad hair. "So is he coming?" Farshad asked.

"I don't know," Cookie said. "I tried. What's this all about?"

"I think I screwed up," Farshad said. He seemed agitated. "Look, I showed those papers Nick got to my parents."

"Willis's mathematical equations," Martina said.

"Right," Farshad said, "*those* papers. And I made it sound like *Ha ha, some nerd gave these to me figuring I wouldn't be able to understand them and wouldn't it be funny if I could*, and then they looked over the papers and it was like I'd shown them the plans for a nuclear bomb or something." He reached up and absentmindedly grabbed a low branch, accidentally snapping it in two with his thumb before letting out a curse.

"Whoa. Put those things away," Cookie said lightly as Farshad looked helplessly at his hands. "So what was in the papers?"

"I don't know," Farshad said. "All they told me was that it was something that they'd been working on for a long time, and the answers that they'd not been able to come up with themselves were in the papers. They were really freaked out, and then demanded to know who'd given me the equations." He fell silent.

"So what did you tell them?" Cookie asked. Farshad looked down at his shoes.

"He told them that Jay was the nerd who had given him the papers to figure out," Martina said.

"Seriously? SERIOUSLY?" Cookie stared at Farshad. "Why would you do that? What is wrong with you?"

"Nothing, nothing," Jay said nonchalantly, emerging from behind a tree. Cookie felt a surge of relief to see him. Her emotions were really all over the place today. "Young sir Rajavi merely had to do some quick thinking and came to the obvious conclusion that I would be the sort of person to give him a math problem for fun. Plus, he probably knew that I'd be able to handle any situation thrown at me."

"Did your parents say anything?" Cookie asked.

"Ah, no, I crept out before there was any sort of confrontation, thanks to your warning. Thank you for that. It really was best for all involved; my parents are not particularly fond of confrontations. Now. What are we going to do?"

"I'm really sorry about this," Farshad started, but Jay waved him off.

"*Phhffftt*, think nothing of it. If they ask me anything I'll just tell them I got the equations from Ms. Zelle. The question is, what are they? And how do they pertain to your particular situation? And how much do your parents know about what's going on at Auxano? And has anyone seen or heard from Nick lately?"

"He's fine," Martina said.

"Oh, good," Jay replied. "Where is he?"

"I have no idea," Martina said.

"Very well, then."

"So this was super fun, and now I have a new thing to add to my ever-growing list of stuff to worry about, but Martina and I need to head out." Cookie brushed a dead leaf off of her skirt.

"Ah, yes, the party!" Jay said. "I'll escort you."

"Uh, excuse me?" Cookie asked with a raised eyebrow.

"The party. I'm coming with you."

"Jay, I don't know if that's such a good idea," Farshad said.

"Why ever not? I scored very high on the exam. So did you! We should both go. You'd need to change, though, you look sweaty."

"Has it occurred to you that we might not be welcome? Because, oh, I don't know, Mike and Eric will be there?"

"And they tried to murder both of you yesterday," Martina pointed out.

"And also you goons are not invited," Cookie said. "Now if you'll excuse us, we'll be heading out."

"But you need us!" Jay said. "How are you going to gather intel while you're at Izaak's house?"

"By being smart and looking dumb," Cookie said. "Not the other way around."

"I . . . I think I'm insulted," Jay said, smiling. Cookie could feel herself gaining some grudging respect for the way that he handled being put down. A guy like Izaak (or his dumb friends) would lash out, or act like they didn't care when it was obvious that they were hurt, but with Jay it was all either mock outrage or water off a duck's back. Nothing seemed to really affect him.

(Well, nothing apart from invading his brain with her anger.)

"You need us there," Jay continued. "Eight eyes are better than four."

"No," Cookie said. "We're not going to watch as you two get into another fight with Mike and Eric. So either you stay here or go . . . wherever to figure out what you're going to do about this whole situation with your parents, and Martina and I will go use our eyes at a party."

Martina's eyes switched quickly from hazel to an almost

unnatural shade of violet. "Glasses, girl," Cookie said. Martina pulled the fake glasses out of her bag and put them on, and they headed out.

Izaak's house wasn't that close to the woods, and Cookie and Martina were already running late. By the time they got there the party was in full swing.

It seemed as though every Company Kid at Deborah Read Middle School had been stuffed into Izaak Marcus's house, as well as some of the parents, who were clustered around the kitchen island. Cookie spied Mike and Eric in a corner, surrounded by other boys and laughing very loud. A few weeks ago, Cookie could have walked straight up to them and pretended to join the fun without missing a beat, but now she felt a shiver of fear run up her spine. For some reason they seemed bigger than before, and meaner.

"We don't have to talk to them," Martina said quietly.

"We should probably listen to what they're talking about, though," Cookie said without moving a muscle to get closer.

Something felt . . . wrong, and Cookie knew without asking that Martina was feeling it as well. The atmosphere was weirdly aggressive, like the time Cookie and her mother had gone with George to his cousin's barbecue. Cookie had noticed her teenage stepsiblings hovering near her mother and her, chatting with forced cheer and offering to walk with them to the bathroom. It had seemed strange at the time, but not as strange as the stares that she'd received from some of George's cousins. They'd left early after George had a tense-seeming talk with one woman, and went straight to the ice cream parlor in Muellersville, because they'd never had the chance to eat anything, and that's when Cookie's stepsister London had given her a taste of pistachio ice cream for the first time. George hadn't spoken to that side of the family since.

It was becoming more and more difficult for Cookie to shut out the thoughts of everyone at the party. She couldn't even make them out clearly; it was just a loud jumble of . . . angry.

"Cookie, Oh Em Gee, you made it!" Claire yelled over the other partygoers, making her way through the crowd to Cookie. "Come come come huggy huggy huggies! And look, here's . . . you!"

"Her name is Martina," Cookie said as Claire brushed past the quiet girl to give Cookie a hug.

"Hi, Martina," Claire said, clearly unsure of whether or not to hug Martina as well. Martina waved at her. "So, girl," Claire said, turning quickly back to Cookie, "I am so glad you're here! I feel like you've dropped off the face of the earth since . . . you know. Since stuff happened."

"Oh, my parents are just freaked and want to keep me close to home," Cookie said. "It'll pass."

"Well, they let you come here," Addison pointed out, sidling up to Cookie and giving her a half hug while completely ignoring Martina.

"I think they were hoping that all your brains would rub off on me," Cookie said, laughing. "Look at all these smart people under one roof!" She could see Izaak trying to balance a decorative poker on his chin by the fireplace of the Marcus family living room. "So much smartness."

"Yeah, his parents are pretty proud," Addison said dryly as the poker fell, knocking several framed photos of Izaak and his older sisters off the mantle.

"He's so talented," Claire breathed.

"At what?" Martina asked.

"At . . . being Izaak," Claire said, irritated.

"Ah," Martina said. "He does seem good at that."

Addison laughed. "You're funny," she told Martina. "Come with me, we're getting something to drink." She grabbed Martina by the arm and steered her toward the kitchen.

Claire watched them go. "I know you're, like, going through stuff because you had a near-death experience and whatnot, but that girl is off, girl."

"Martina?" Cookie asked as she watched Jordan Dameroff try to crack whole walnuts with his bare hands. "She's fine. She's just quiet."

"Sure," Claire said. "Look, if you like her, then she must

be cool. But it's weird that you're hanging out with her instead of us, your real, actual friends."

"I'm not hanging out with her instead of you," Cookie said, annoyed. She was beginning to realize that the noise of the party was amplified by the din of the thoughts of the partygoers, and she had to tamp down a sudden, desperate need to be around the only person at the party who knew what she was going through. But that person had just left to get drinks with Addison. "Get a grip," she told Claire.

"A grip?" Claire said, her voice rising. "A grip?!?"

"Yes, *girl*, a grip," Cookie said. Claire was looking a little crazy. "I can hang out with who I want to hang out with. And me having another friend doesn't make us not friends. Unless you've gone completely mental."

"I AM NOT MENTAL!" Claire screamed, and with a quick movement she punched a hole in the wall, directly under a framed portrait of Izaak's older sister and her prom date. Everyone else at the party stopped talking to look at them.

"Oh my god," Cookie said, her eyes widening as she stared at Claire's fist, or at the wall around her fist.

"I didn't mean to do that," Claire said, and started to cry. Izaak's mother rushed over to see what had happened and let out a small shriek.

"I'M SO SORRY!" Claire wailed as Dr. Marcus gently extricated her fist from the wall. "IT WAS AN ACCIDENT!"

Her small hand was covered in plaster dust and her knuckles were raw and bloody. She continued to sob as Dr. Marcus brought her into the kitchen, saying, "I know, I know. Let's get you cleaned up, okay?"

"So, is this something that usually happens at parties?" Martina asked, handing Cookie a red plastic cup of purple soda. "I don't know if I like parties."

Cookie looked at the hole in the wall. "She did that because she was mad at me. Let's get out of here."

"I thought we wanted to look for evidence that the high test scorers had taken Dr. Deery's formula."

Cookie looked at the hole again, and then at the group of Auxano parents that were clustered around Claire. They were talking in low voices and had worried looks on their faces. "I think we found it."

"What did you find?" Izaak asked, sidling up to them. He looked at the hole in the wall. "Holy sh—"

"Claire likes you," Martina told him.

"What?" Izaak looked confused. "Claire likes me?"

WHAT ARE YOU DOING?

"Sure," Martina said. "You should go ask her how she's doing."

"She . . . she punched a hole in my wall."

"I know," Cookie said, thinking fast, "how cool is that?"

"I guess it's pretty badass," Izaak said, slowly nodding his head. "And she likes me?"

"Yes," Martina said.

STOP TELLING HIM THAT!

"That's . . . cool," Izaak said. "Wait, who are you?"

"You should probably go see how she's doing," Cookie said.

"Right," Izaak said, and headed to the kitchen where his mom was putting an ice pack on Claire's injured hand.

Cookie turned to Martina. "Why did you tell him that?" she hissed.

"Because it's true," Martina said.

"So?"

"So it made him go away."

"Well, yes, but . . ." Cookie pressed her fingers to her temples. "Look, you don't just tell someone that someone else likes them. That's not your information to give. She's going to be so embarrassed and then she's going to kill us, which, judging by the way she just punched through a wall, she could probably actually do."

"Oh. But he likes her."

"How do you even know that?"

Martina shrugged.

"We need to get out of here," Cookie said, turning to head out the door.

"Hey!" Addison rushed up to them. "Where are you going? And what did you say to Claire?"

"Hi, Addison," Martina said, gently inserting herself between Addison and Cookie.

"Hi. What did you say to Claire?" Addison asked over Martina's shoulder.

The other thoughts in Cookie's head were getting difficult to tune out. One of the parents was wondering about the fastest way to get to a hospital, and another was wondering about the best way to get to Auxano. Emma was wondering if she should go and talk to Claire, and Eric and Mike were wondering if they could punch bigger holes in the walls than Claire had. And Addison was still trying to get around Martina to confront Cookie.

"What did you do?" Addison was asking.

"I didn't do anything, she just freaked out," Cookie said, feeling weak.

"You did do something, otherwise she wouldn't have done . . . THIS!" Addison shouted, pointing to the damaged wall.

"Maybe make her go away?" Martina asked Cookie, but it was all Cookie could do to remain standing upright. There were too many people, too many thoughts, and the room was spinning.

"WHAT DOES THAT MEAN, MAKE ME GO AWAY?"

Addison screamed, her face twisted with rage. Cookie had never seen her friend act this way. She'd never seen anyone act this way.

"I think we need to go now," Martina said as Addison raised her fist. She was not aiming for the wall, though. She was aiming at them.

"GAH! RIHANNA!" Nick yelped. He was right next to them, and he was holding a live, squawking, flapping chicken.

FARSHAD AND JAY WERE SLOWLY WALKING. NOR-mally they were both fast walkers; Farshad was a runner and he had long legs, and Jay was naturally hyper, yet despite that they were walking very, very slow without any real sense of where they were headed.

"We should follow the girls," Jay said. "But at a safe distance."

"And then what?" Farshad asked. "We hide in the bushes outside of Izaak Marcus's house?"

"Don't be silly, we don't even know if he has bushes. And you're very tall—and, I suspect, bad at hiding." Jay thought a moment. "Maybe they have a tree we can climb."

"No," Farshad said. "That is not happening."

"Oh, come on, when's the last time you climbed a tree?"

"Okay, let's say we get there, and we somehow manage to find a tree to climb, what then? We just hang out in a tree outside of a party that we're not invited to so we can sort of peek through the windows?"

"I may not have thought this through enough," Jay muttered. They continued to walk.

Farshad didn't want to go home. Home was where his parents were and with them more questions that he had no idea how to answer. "Are you going to tell your parents that Ms. Zelle gave you the papers?" he asked Jay.

"If I have to, although I'm beginning to think that maybe that isn't the best idea. She's pretty embedded in Auxano. They may actually ask her about it."

"How much do you think they know?"

"How much do you think your parents know?"

"How much do *we* actually know?" Farshad wondered.

"Not enough." Jay had a sudden look of determination on his face. "But I know who does. We need to get to a computer." He looked at Farshad. "That you haven't ruined."

"Okay, why?"

"Because we need to find . . . THE HAMMER."

"Did you seriously just pause for dramatic effect?"

"I . . . DID. Did it work?"

"Kind of."

"Bully for me! So here's the plan. We email The Hammer to set up a meeting so we can find out what he knows and compare notes. Then, if anything happens to us, at least we'll have a reputable journalist who knows our story."

"Jay. The Hammer is a conspiracy blogger. That's pretty much the exact opposite of a reputable journalist."

"But is it?"

"Yes! It is!"

"Oh, but is it?"

"Is this how you win arguments? You just wear your opponent down?"

"You'd be amazed at how effective it is. Let's go find a computer!"

Farshad threw up his hands. "Fine. But just because I don't want to go home. And you probably *shouldn't* go home. Does Nick have a computer we can use?"

"His aunts do. Let's go."

"Is he there?"

"Sure!"

"Oh. I thought you didn't know where he was."

"I don't."

"Then why did you say, 'Sure!'?"

"Because, my treelike friend," Jay said, spinning on his heel to face Farshad, and reaching up to grasp both of his shoulders, "sometimes you just have to act like you know what you're doing in order to get anything done. Why am I always the only one who seems to know this? Besides Cookie." He let go and started walking in the direction of Molly and Jilly's house. "Let's find Nick."

NICK HAD NEVER RUN SO FAST IN HIS LIFE. HE HAD NO idea where he was, or where he was going, but he was very, very aware that it would be best to get away from the horde of deranged partygoers that seemed intent on tearing Rihanna limb from limb. And possibly him as well. Probably him as well.

It seemed that Martina had taken charge, choosing which direction to run. She had grabbed Cookie's hand, which seemed to be the only thing keeping the smaller girl moving. They zigged and zagged through the evening suburban streets as fast as they could go, but Nick could hear the party crowd behind them. They were a mob. A crazed, bloodthirsty, potentially chicken-murdery mob.

"This way," Martina said quickly, ducking into a darkened yard and rolling under a split-rail fence, dragging Cookie behind her. Nick's eyes widened. There was no way he was fitting under there.

"THEY WENT THIS WAY!" Nick heard someone who was much too close to them shout, and all of a sudden he and Rihanna were on the other side of the fence. He took off after Martina and Cookie.

They ran and ran, through backyards and small wooded areas, until they could no longer hear the mob behind them. Nick collapsed on the ground near a small residential construction site. He felt like his lungs were about to burst, and he let go of Rihanna. The chicken wandered around non-chalantly, as if she hadn't been through both teleportation and a mad chase, and started pecking at a discarded fast-food bag near a dumpster. Martina and Cookie were also breathing hard, but managed to stay mostly upright.

"Why . . ." Nick wheezed, "why is a mob of Company Kids chasing us?"

"Why are you carrying a chicken?" Martina asked, watching Rihanna down a half-eaten French fry. "Is it like the bunnies? Is it a screaming chicken?"

"Bok," Rihanna said.

"I guess not," Martina said.

"No, no, I was just trying to see if I could teleport with something that was alive," Nick explained.

"Bok," Rihanna said.

"Sorry, *someone* alive." Nick looked over at Cookie, who was doubled over and clutching her head. "Cookie. Are you all right?"

Cookie shook her head.

"She was a little overwhelmed in there," Martina explained.

"I thought you were getting better at tuning people out," Nick said, awkwardly patting Cookie's back.

"I was," she said, "but those were not normal thoughts." She looked up at Martina. "Did you see the look on Addison's face when she was about to hit me?"

"I did," Martina said quietly.

"I know you're not exactly the resident expert on normal, but did that seem normal to you?" Cookie asked.

"No," Martina said. "She looked like a crazed ragebeast."

"Claire looked the same way, right before she punched the wall," Cookie said.

"And Eric looked that way when he was threatening to kill Neil deGrasse Hamster."

"And how that entire crowd of Company Kids looked when they were trying to kill us right now?" Nick asked.

"And their thoughts—they were just really . . . angry," Cookie said. "And they were all thinking them at once."

"Do you still hear them?"

"A little," Cookie admitted. "I want it to stop."

"Just breathe," Martina told her. She looked at Nick. "Do you think you could teleport with us?" she asked him.

"I don't know," he said. "That's the goal, but as it is I barely teleported with Rihanna."

"You named the chicken Rihanna?" Cookie asked.

"Bok," Rihanna bokked, and cocked her head toward a sound in the distance.

It was the angry mob of Company Kids, and from the sound of it they weren't just looking for them anymore. Nick could hear sounds of smashing windows and splintering wood. He grabbed Rihanna.

"What are they doing?" Cookie whispered.

"I do not want to find out," Nick whispered back, looking around wildly. They were surrounded by fencing and the only way out was back toward the sound of the melee.

"Here!" Martina pointed to a large dumpster and began to run toward it.

"You're kidding me," Nick heard Cookie moan as he ran past her.

"It's fine, it's mostly empty!" Martina called from inside the dumpster. About a half second later Nick and Rihanna were in there with her, having unintentionally teleported through the side of it. There were some splintered two-by-four planks of wood and the floor was unpleasantly sticky, but otherwise it seemed fine. Cookie peeked her head over the edge.

"Gross," she said despairingly, "gross gross gross and I hate this and I hate both of you for making me do this gross gross gross."

"Come on!" Nick shoved Rihanna into Martina's arms and went to help Cookie. "Jump, I'll catch you!"

"Gross!" she whimpered, and tumbled into him. His catching skills were less than stellar and they tumbled to the bottom of the dumpster. Cookie used his body to push herself into an upright position without having to touch the sticky floor. She was on the verge of saying something (probably "gross"), but Martina put her finger to her lips. They quietly moved to the most shadowy corner of the dumpster and crouched together as the Company Kids gathered outside.

Nick tried to listen for distinct voices, but he couldn't hear any. He couldn't even hear distinct words—the Company Kids seemed to be just screaming in rage and banging things into other things. They sounded like wild animals. Really pissed-off wild animals. Nick looked at Cookie, who was holding her hands over her head and shaking with actual terror. Martina, too, looked uncharacteristically scared, her wide eyes changing from light blue to dark gray to brown to green to hazel with maddening speed that only got faster as the Company Kids began to bang on the side of the dumpster.

"BOK!" Rihanna said.

There was no way that they had heard her over the sounds of their own banging and wailing. Someone screamed something that sounded vaguely like an order to continue the hunt elsewhere, and the banging stopped as the Company Kids made their way out of the construction site. Nick slowly let out the breath that he hadn't realized he'd been holding in.

"BOK BOK BOK BOK BOK BOK BOKBOKBOKBOK!!!" Rihanna screamed, and Nick, Cookie, and Martina clung to one another in terror as the mob thundered back.

Claire's face popped over the edge of the dumpster, wild-eyed with fury. She spotted the terrified trio and threw back her head and let out a long, ear-splitting shriek, and Nick desperately wished to be anywhere other than stuck in a sticky dumpster surrounded by bloodthirsty maniacs.

"It worked!" Abe said, delighted. "Hello, Martina, hello, Cookie, good to see you."

"Bok," Rihanna said.

FARSHAD WAS UNCOMFORTABLE. IN ADDITION TO not being accustomed to hanging out at other people's houses, he really wasn't accustomed to hanging out at other people's houses when they weren't even there. Added to that was the extra layer of weird that he and Jay weren't even at Nick's house; they were at his aunts' house. So they were uninvited guests of a guest that wasn't even there. Jay seemed completely unbothered by the situation.

"Where did you say Nick was again?" Nick's mom asked as she brought Farshad and Jay some chocolate milk. "It's getting pretty late for him to be out by himself."

"Nonsense, my dearest Angela," Jay said, enthusiastically slurping his chocolate milk while he opened her laptop without asking. "Nick just had to return some books to the library."

"The library is closed."

"He's using the drop box. Terrific invention, without which he would have accrued a fine, and no one wants that."

"I thought you said he needed the books for the research project you're doing. Which is why you needed my computer."

"No, no, he was returning other books so that he could return tomorrow to get new books for the research project. Don't worry, he should be here any moment." Jay was typing furiously into the computer. Farshad felt a sudden jealousy—he remembered when he had been able to type fast without needing to be hyper careful to not destroy the keyboard.

"Angela?" Jilly called from the kitchen. "Is Molly home yet?"

"Not yet, hon, she just texted to tell me that she's stuck in traffic on 222, there's some sort of accident or something." Angela looked worriedly at the clock. "I'm giving Nick twenty minutes," she told Jay, "and then I'm heading out to look for him."

"I wish you wouldn't worry. Nick is a strapping young buck."

Angela stifled a laugh and headed to the kitchen. Farshad waited for her to be out of earshot and leaned closer to Jay.

"Why did you tell her that?" he whispered. "We have no idea where Nick even is!"

Jay dismissed him with a wave of his hand. "He'll turn up eventually."

"He could be anywhere! He could be in Timbuktu!"

"That seems unlikely. From what I gather he tends to end up in a place or with a person he's been thinking about, and if I know Nick, which I do, Timbuktu hasn't ever been that high up on that list." Jay turned the laptop toward Far-shad. "Here, does this seem in order to you?"

Jay had found the contact page on The Hammer's website and left a dramatic message about the bus accident, Auxano, and their suspicions about the Company Kids. He'd left out their names, but it was still disturbing to Farshad to see all of his recent personal turmoil spelled out in a few paragraphs. "I don't know, Jay . . ." he started.

Jay clicked the Send button. "Done!"

"I . . . I was just saying that I didn't know if this is a good idea!"

"Second-guessing is for the birds," Jay said. "Actually, birds probably don't second-guess themselves. Second-guessing is for humans. Let's be more like birds."

"Birds fly into sliding glass doors all the time."

"We should be like smarter birds, then." Jay looked up from the computer. "I wonder how long it will take for him to get back to us. I imagine he's a really busy guy."

"That's funny, I imagined the exact opposite." From across the living room Farshad heard a sharp cry. He and Jay stood up.

"Okay, okay, okay," Angela was telling Jilly as she led her out of the kitchen and into the living room. "I'm going to get your bag. Do you need to sit down?"

"NO," Jilly roared. She was clutching her pregnant belly

and her breathing was heavy. "TALL KID, WALK ME TO THE CAR."

It took Farshad a moment to realize that she was talking to him. "YES, YOU," Jilly yelled. "CAR. WALK ME. NOW." He rushed over to her and she leaned on him as they made their way out the door to the driveway.

"CALL MOLLY," Jilly wailed as she heaved herself into the backseat of Nick's mom's car. Angela and Jay hurried out with Jilly's packed bag.

"Okay," Angela said, sliding into the driver's seat. "We are going to the hospital. Jay, you hold down the fort and when Nick gets home you tell him to meet us there. Here is money for dinner"—she shoved two twenties into Jay's hand—"and you have my phone number. You call when he comes home and I'll order him a car to take him to the hospital. You got that?"

"I will endeavor—"

"HE'S GOT IT. HE IS ON TOP OF THIS. WE ARE GO-ING," Jilly belted from the backseat.

"We're going! Everyone is staying calm! Everything is great! JAY, YOU PROMISE TO CALL ME!" Angela yelled as they backed out of the driveway.

"I PROMISE!" Jay yelled back, and then they were standing alone in front of the house.

"This is turning into a very weird evening," Farshad said, and thought for a beat. "Another very weird evening."

"Let's see if The Hammer wrote back!" Jay said, dashing back into Molly and Jilly's house. Farshad followed him.

"He wrote back! He wrote back!!!" Jay yelped with awed delight a moment later. "He wants to meet up! Should I tell him to come here?"

"No!" Farshad exclaimed. "You can't invite a total stranger to meet up at the house of your friend's aunt who has just gone into labor and trusted you to be alone in her house."

"Who says?"

"ANY. GOOD. HUMAN. BEING."

"Yikes strikes, man, calm yourself, I won't have him come here. But this puts us in a bit of a pickle, because Angela has entrusted me to stay here and wait for Nick." Jay paced back and forth in front of the coffee table with the open laptop on it. "Pickle pickle pickle."

"Look, we just can't go. You made a promise. We have to stay here."

Jay stopped pacing. "Actually, that's not technically true."

"I was there." Farshad sighed. "I heard you."

"Yes, I did promise I'd stay here, but you made no such promise. You, my very tall extraordinarily be-thumbed friend, are going to have to go alone."

"What? No."

"I know, I know, I'm as disappointed as you are that I can't come along. But someone has to go, and clearly it can't be me."

Farshad looked at the clock. "My parents are going to freak out if I don't get home soon," he said. "And they're going to super freak out if I get murdered by some weirdo conspiracy theorist that I foolishly met up with in the middle of the night."

Jay gasped. "I GASP AT YOU!" he said. "The Hammer would never murder you in the middle of the night, or any other time. He is a speaker of truths and a warrior for righteousness, not a murderer of extremely tall almost-teenagers. Here" — he sat on the sofa and started to type — "I'll tell him to meet up outside of the ice cream shop. It's public and well-lit. Just email your parents and tell them that you got stuck at Nick's because his mom had to take his aunt to the hospital, and then you can go."

"I like exactly none of this," Farshad growled.

"Pish-posh, get over it," Jay said. "Just get there and find out what he knows. The more information we have, the better prepared we'll be to deal with whatever comes next."

"You are a freaky little dude, you know that, right?"

"I'm well aware. Off you go!"

COOKIE LOOKED AROUND, BEWILDERED. NO MORE banging, no more screaming, no more sticky dumpster, and most of all, no more rage thoughts permeating her brain. "Oh my god," she whispered. "Oh my god oh my god oh my god."

"Nick," Martina said, "you did it."

Nick half leaned, half fell into a bale of hay in the barn where they found themselves. "And all it took was the complete terror of being hunted down by a roving band of deranged middle-school overachievers." He hugged the chicken he'd named Rihanna closer to him.

"What happened?" Abe asked at the same time that Cookie asked, "Where are we?" They looked at each other for a moment before Abe relented.

"You are in my neighbor's barn and that is my chicken. I can take you back into town unless . . ." He looked at Nick expectantly.

"I am pretty sure that I shouldn't try that again until I can control where I'm going," Nick said. "I don't want to zap us right back to the roving band of deranged middle-school overachievers."

"I would prefer not to do that," Martina chimed in.

"Me, three," Cookie said. "I never want to see any of those lunatics ever again."

"Who is a lunatic? Who are we talking about?" Abe asked.

"Remember how we suspected that the kids of the people who worked for Auxano were being given the same formula that made us get these superpowers?"

"The poison they gave to Rebecca and the others, of course."

"Well, we think it's made them kind of violently crazy and they've formed a mob and are running around Muellersville destroying stuff," Nick told him.

"And you are sure this is not something they normally do?"

"Pretty sure."

"We should probably stop them," Martina said, "before they actually hurt anyone."

"What are you going to do, change your eye color at them?" Cookie snapped.

"Do you think that would stop them?" Martina asked. "I don't think it would. We probably need a better plan."

"Their parents should be stopping them!" Cookie exploded. "It's their fault! They did this to their own kids and it made them into freaky monsters and it's all because they wanted them to do well on some stupid tests and they need to stop it!"

She glared furiously at everyone in the barn. "Well? How is this our job?"

Abe took a step toward her. "Because we can," he said, his voice full of resolve.

The barn was silent.

"So?" Cookie asked, very annoyed. "That is not an answer. I CAN do lots of stuff that I don't do all the time. Now, please, if you don't mind, I don't trust Blinky Boy over there to zap us home, so I'm going to have to ask for another ride in the horse buggy of death to get back into town."

"All right," Abe said, his shoulders slumped. He looked at Nick. "You're going to have to leave the chicken."

"Bok," Rihanna said.

Wait, if I leave Rihanna here what happens to her?
What do you mean?
Is she an egg sort of chicken or a... barbecue sort of chicken?
I do not know. She is a chicken. She is not your chicken. Leave the chicken.
Promise me she won't get eaten.
No.
I'm taking the chicken.
Bok!

FARSHAD WAITED OUTSIDE THE ICE CREAM PARLOR, feeling ill at ease. It was bad enough that he was supposed to be meeting up with some weirdo who was probably going to think Farshad was a terrorist the moment he saw him, but he also had a weird feeling in general. After about ten minutes of sitting on the bench outside the parlor Farshad realized why—besides the two bored teenagers working behind the ice cream counter, he hadn't seen anyone else.

No one was walking down the street. No one else was in the ice cream parlor. There were hardly any cars driving by. The whole town was eerily silent and still.

Jay had lent Farshad his watch (while pleading with him to please try not thumb-crushing it). It was still early enough that Farshad's parents shouldn't have been too worried, but Farshad knew that they were, seeing how serious and almost frightened they'd become when they saw Willis's computations. Maybe he should just blow off this whole stupid meeting ("It's a rendezvous!" Farshad almost heard Jay saying in his head) and go home. Answer any questions in as vague a way as possible, sleep in his own bed, and let everything just sort itself out. Yes. That's what he should do.

Farshad heard a crashing sound in the distance, as if someone had thrown a metal trash can into a car or something. He heard a car alarm go off. And there was another noise as well . . . people. Loud people in a group. Farshad stood up and looked down the street to get a better view.

It was the Company Kids who were supposed to be at the party where Cookie and Martina were supposed to be. Addison was leading the group, and as she passed under a street lamp Farshad could see that she was carrying something that looked like a stick or a pipe. Behind her a lot of the Company Kids seemed to be carrying the sort of stuff you'd find lying around a construction site—Eric Mathes had a two-by-four.

They were still pretty far away, and Farshad took a step toward them, hoping to hear what they were saying. It took a minute for him to realize they weren't saying anything.

They were just making noises.

Screamy noises.

Farshad quickly looked around for a shadow to hide in, but he was in the center of town and everything was entirely too well-lit. Farshad turned back to see Addison raising what he could now see was a lead pipe and smashing it down on the windshield of a parked car. A victorious roar went up from the crowd behind her.

Farshad grabbed the handle to the ice cream parlor door and tried to open it, but it was locked. The two teenagers who were working inside were standing right there with their faces pressed up against the glass, looking with terror at the oncoming mob. "Let me in!" he whispered as loud as he dared, pulling in vain at the door.

"ZOMBIES!" one of them screamed.

"Are you kidding me?!?" Farshad hissed through clenched teeth. "Let me in!"

"NO THANK YOU!" the teen screamed.

The next voice came from down the street. "TERROR BOY!!!"

Farshad looked up. The good news was that the Company Kids could still use actual words instead of just random primal screams. The bad news was that they had spotted him and now they were all yelling, "TERROR BOY! TERROR BOY! TERROR BOOOOOYYYYY!!!"

"YOU GUYS SUCK!" Farshad yelled at the ice cream parlor employees before turning and running down the street away from the howling Company Kids.

Farshad knew he was fast, but as he ran it occurred to him that it was entirely possible that Dr. Deery's formula had given one of the Company Kids super speed or teleportation like Nick's. He could be beating his best running time just to hurl himself smack-dab into his enemy. He focused thoughts at Cookie as he ran, desperately hoping that she would somehow be able to hear him and find a way to help.

"KID, GET IN!" A maroon minivan was driving alongside Farshad, and the sliding back door was open. The driver was a pale, balding guy who looked like he was in his thirties.

"NO!" Farshad yelled, running harder.

"KID, I AM TRYING TO HELP YOU!" the guy shouted. "GET IN THE CAR!"

"NO THANK YOU!" Farshad yelled back, pushing himself to run faster. They were in the middle of the block and there were no other roads or alleys for him to duck into.

"GROOVY! GROOVY!" the guy yelled. It was the code word that Jay had set up so that Farshad would recognize The Hammer.

"TERROR BOOOOYYEEEEEEEE!" The Company Kids were getting closer. He could either get into a car with a complete stranger who might be mentally unstable or face a large crowd of bloodthirsty racists who were definitely mentally unstable. He should have gone home when he had the chance.

"FINE!" he yelled, and The Hammer slowed his car down just enough for Farshad to open the door and throw himself into the backseat, immediately becoming entangled in two toddler car seats that took up the entire bench. "GO GO GO!" he gasped as someone chucked a two-by-four at them. Another one bounced off the rear bumper.

"STRAP IN!" The Hammer yelled.

"THAT IS IMPOSSIBLE, I AM NOT THREE!"

The Hammer muttered a few choice curse words as something else hit his minivan. "Get in the front seat!" he yelled, and Farshad scrambled to get his long legs over the cup holders and armrests to get situated. He fumbled to get belted in, which was really tricky to do without his thumbs. But he couldn't trust himself to not break the man's car.

"I'm in!" he said when he heard the click, and The Hammer slammed his foot on the gas pedal, quickly leaving the horde of angry high scorers far behind them. Farshad slumped in his seat. "Where are we going?"

"I don't know, I don't know, I don't know," The Hammer said anxiously. "What have I done, what have I done, what have I done?"

"What? What did you do?" Farshad asked, feeling the strength in his thumbs. He did still have them. If push came to shove, he could use them.

"I don't know how old you are but you have got to be under seventeen and I have no idea who you are and oh my god, I think I'm a kidnapper!" The Hammer was sweating profusely. "But I couldn't just leave you there, could I? They were going to kill you! But you also shouldn't be in my car. Because I might have just kidnapped you."

"How about you drive me home, and then you will not be a kidnapper anymore?" Farshad said with care.

"Of course! Of course. Yes. Very good." The Hammer ran a hand through his thinning hair. "You know, I had this whole plan that I was going to park around the corner and then meet you and pretend to be The Hammer's lawyer so you wouldn't know my secret identity, but then I saw this mob of kids—kids!—just screaming and smashing everything and then I saw them chasing you and I saw how those jerks at the ice cream place wouldn't let you in and I couldn't just leave you, could I? And then I said 'Groovy' and I realized who you were and WHAT WAS UP WITH THOSE KIDS? What was happening? Do you know?"

Farshad eyed The Hammer. He'd learned over the years to never give more information than was absolutely necessary, because that information could be used against you in the future. You tell someone that your parents are Iranian? A few years later everyone would think you were a terrorist. Farshad was not inclined to tell this panicking man in a minivan all of his deepest darkest secrets and the crazy stuff he'd seen and learned over the past few weeks.

But Jay's parting words nagged at him. "Tell him everything," Jay had said, "because he's the only one who is going to believe us and someone should know the whole story. You know. In case anything happens."

Farshad had rolled his eyes at Jay's paranoia, but that was before he'd been chased by a mob of crazed middle-school classmates; now anything was possible. He looked out the window and saw that they were driving down a street where every several car windshields had been smashed in. "What is happening?" The Hammer asked again, this time in a quiet, terrified whisper.

"Okay," Farshad said, "I'm going to tell you everything that I know, but you have to keep all names anonymous, okay?" The Hammer nodded vigorously, his hands gripped tightly to the steering wheel. "And you're taking me home first," he added, giving The Hammer directions.

They passed a few more blocks of smashed-up cars and mailboxes. "Where are the police?" Farshad asked.

"Where is anyone?" The Hammer asked back. They were the only moving car on the road. "Do you think they've all been . . . taken?"

"What? Taken where? Nobody's been taken." Farshad looked into the windows of the houses as they drove slowly down the eerily quiet street. "Look, that guy's watching wrestling in his underwear."

"But is he really?" The Hammer asked suspiciously.

"I'd rather not look at the half-naked guy again, if that's cool with you. Nobody's been taken." Farshad saw the head-lights of a car in the distance. "See? Another car."

It was a white van, and it was driving very, very fast toward them, and suddenly it was so close that Farshad could see the white-hazmat-suited people driving it before it blew right past them. It was the same kind of white van with the same hazmat suits that had taken Mr. Friend away.

"Oh no," Farshad said.

"What? What? Who were those guys?"

"They were the people who take people away. Turn around! Follow them!"

"This is a terrible idea!" The Hammer said as he clumsily turned the car around to follow the van. "Oh my god oh my god oh my god ARE THEY ALIENS?"

"What? No!"

"Then who are they and why are they taking people and where are they taking them?!?"

"They're scientists from Auxano who have genetically or chemically altered some of the kids at school so that they'd do better at tests and now the kids are freaking out so the scientists are going to imprison them in the labs, just like they did Mr. Friend!"

"I KNEW IT!" The Hammer screamed as he sped down the residential road.

"No, you didn't, you just asked me if they were aliens."

"I'M VERY FRIGHTENED."

"Slow down, slow down, they're slowing down, we don't want them to see us." Farshad could see the mob of Company Kids in the distance, and he could hear them howling like predators at the approaching white van.

"Oh," The Hammer whispered, "I am definitely keeping my distance." He parked in the shadow of a large tree. "Do you really think that they're going to just grab them? How? There's not enough room in the van for all those kids." He took out his cell phone, pointed at the scene, and began to record. "This is THE HAMMER," he said in a completely different, much more gravelly voice, "and I'm here in the heart of Muellersville. What you're seeing is some local kids who have been given MIND-ALTERING SUBSTANCES by the Auxano Corporation and set loose to cause destruction and mayhem. I have seen smashed-up cars, assaulted mailboxes, and I personally saved one young boy from becoming the prey of . . . THE HOWLING ZOMBIES OF DEBORAH READ MIDDLE SCHOOL."

"Seriously?" Farshad hissed.

"That was the voice of the boy I saved. He's very frightened . . ." The Hammer's rough voice trailed off. "Look, look, another one!" he whispered in terror.

From around a corner came another white van, and then another, and another, until there were seven vans surrounding the Company Kids, who snarled and screamed.

And then they attacked the vans.

"Oh nooooo!" The Hammer squealed in an alarmingly high-pitched voice.

Then there was smoke—someone in a white hazmat suit had lobbed some sort of smoke bomb into the crowd, and the Company Kids dropped their weapons and began to violently cough. Some doubled over, and a few seemed to pass out. The white hazmats poured out of the seven vans and systematically grabbed the kids and put them in the vans. Once every last kid was in, the doors were shut and the vans all disappeared in a line down the road. The whole thing took less than a minute.

The Hammer put his phone down. "What do we do . . . Do we follow them?"

"No," Farshad said. He felt like he was going to throw up. "We know where they're going."

**ICK HELD TIGHT TO RIHANNA AS THEY TRAVELED IN** Abe's buggy through the cornfields and grazing pastures that surrounded Muellersville. He had absolutely no idea what he was going to do with a chicken once he got home. His mom was going to think he'd lost his mind. Maybe if he could learn to focus his power he could teleport Rihanna to somewhere safe . . .

"I just got service," Cookie said. She was looking at her phone. "My parents are freaking out." She looked up at Nick and Martina. "There are news reports of a major gas leak in Muellersville and everyone is strongly encouraged to stay in their homes until the leak is contained." She started texting back to her parents.

"A gas leak?" Nick asked. "Since when?"

"Since a mob of out-of-control kids started destroying everything in their path," Martina said.

"Are you saying that there is no gas leak? That it's all a cover-up?"

"Possibly."

"Can they do that?" Nick was aghast.

"I don't know. But it's weird that a gas leak is happening right at the same time that a mob of out-of-control kids are destroying everything in their path."

Nick looked at Martina. Her insights never failed to surprise him. "So, what do we do?"

"My mom wants me to stay at the party until the threat is over," Cookie said. "Because she still thinks I'm at the party." She held out her phone to Martina. "Do you need to call your parents?"

"No."

"Oh no, my mom," Nick said. Cookie handed him her phone.

"Nick!" His mother sounded frantic. "What number is this? Where are you?"

"I . . . I ran into my friend . . . Martina, and she lent me her phone to call you."

"Where are you? Are you at her house? Are you still at the library?"

The library? What? "We're just walking down the street on our way home," he said, hoping desperately that his mother couldn't hear the sounds of the moving buggy, or of Rihanna's clucking. It was not quiet.

"Nick, listen to me, you have to get inside! There's some sort of gas leak emergency and it's not safe to be out and about. I'm with Jilly at the hospital, and the police and the hazardous materials guys blocked off so many roads that it took us forever to get here and Molly is still trying to make her way over, so this is SERIOUS. Get home!"

"Is Jilly having the baby?!?"

"Yes, sweetie, yes, look, I have to go, get home, Jay is

there, keep him there, call his parents, just—I'm coming, I'm coming, Nick is fine, he's with some girl . . . I don't know what girl, a girl—just get back to Molly and Jilly's and get inside, okay? And call me when you're safe."

Nick handed the phone back to Cookie. "Why did you tell your mom it was Martina's phone?" she asked.

"I don't know. I panicked."

"Are you ashamed to be talking on my phone?" Cookie asked. She looked mad.

"No! It's just that it's easier for me to say I was with Martina because my mom doesn't know who Martina is. Everyone knows who you are."

"Because I'm black?"

"Well, yes, and because you're named after a pastry. And because you're the most popular girl in the school and it doesn't make sense that the most popular girl in the school is hanging out with me."

Cookie leaned back, folded her arms over her chest, and looked out the window. "Well, I used to be the most popular girl in the school. I'm pretty sure that isn't true anymore, seeing how all my friends want to murder me."

"Oh," Martina said, "I think they want to murder everyone. You're not special."

"Thanks, Martina," Cookie growled.

"Sure."

"Hey," Nick said suddenly, "does anyone know where Farshad is?"

"Oh, we meant to tell you, he—"

And all of a sudden, Cookie disappeared. And so did Martina. And so did the whole buggy.

"AAAAAAHHHHH!!!!" a thin-haired man screamed from the driver's seat of the moving vehicle where Nick found himself.

"BOK!" bokked Rihanna.

Oh. They hadn't disappeared, Nick realized, seeing Farshad in the passenger's seat of what seemed to be a minivan. *He* had. The driver continued to scream.

"SHUT UP AND LOOK AT THE ROAD!" Farshad commanded, and the man stopped making noises, even though his mouth continued to hang open. "Oh, hey, Nick."

"Hey."

"I see you have a chicken there."

"Her name is Rihanna."

"Does she have any dangerous superpowers?"

"Nope, she's just a chicken."

"Okay."

"WHAT IS HAPPENING?" The man at the wheel looked like he was about to cry, and Nick couldn't blame him. When a twelve-year-old and a chicken randomly beam into your minivan you get to freak out.

"Mr. . . . Hammer, this is a friend," Farshad explained. "Nick, this is The Hammer."

"You mean the blogger?"

"You've read my work?" The Hammer asked hopefully.

"Sure," Nick said, catching Farshad's eye.

Farshad shrugged. "Jay made me meet up with him."

That explained a lot. "Of course. So . . . where are we going?"

"I am taking you boys home," The Hammer said, a note of hysteria in his voice. "Can you put on a seat belt, please?"

The backseat was taken up by little-kid car seats, but Nick decided not to argue with the strange man who was suddenly driving him around, and with some effort he wedged himself between the two bulky seats.

"Wait, slow down," Farshad said. Up the road Nick could see a white van that was toppled over on its side. The back doors were wide open.

"Oh no," The Hammer breathed, stopping next to the overturned van.

It was a mess. There were skid marks on the road, and Nick could see scratches and indentations where someone (or many people) inside had kicked and punched their way out of the back compartment. Thankfully there was no blood.

"The driver is still in the car!" The Hammer said. "And someone else! What do we do?"

"We have to get them out!" Nick said, bolting out the door and ducking down to look through the windshield. "Are they alive?"

"Let me, let me," Farshad said as he approached, hooking his thumbs around the windshield and pulling it off the van as if it were made of tinfoil. Behind them, The Hammer fainted. "Check on him."

The Hammer seemed okay. "Get his phone, it's charging in the minivan!" Farshad commanded. "And call for an ambulance!" He was dragging the driver and the passenger out through the hole where the windshield had been. They were both wearing white hazmat suits.

Nick set Rihanna down by The Hammer and ran to get the phone, quickly calling 911 and giving them the street name. Back at the van Farshad was taking the hoods off of two injured Auxano goons. Nick heard Farshad let out a little gasp and he ran back to him.

The driver of the van was Dr. Deery. The passenger was Ms. Zelle. She moaned without opening her eyes. Farshad and Nick both took an involuntary step backward.

"What do we do?" Nick asked. "We can't just leave them here."

"But we can't let them see us, either," Farshad whispered. "Did you call the ambulance?"

"They said they're on their way. How did this happen?"

"The Company Kids went berserk at that party. Dr. Deery's formula is making them completely insane." Farshad looked up at the busted van. "And strong. The Auxano guys came to pick them up."

"So they escaped?"

"The ones in this van did. There were six other vans." Ms. Zelle moaned again. "We have to get out of here."

In the distance Nick could hear a siren approaching. "What about that guy?" he asked, looking at The Hammer.

"He's crazy. Let's go! Can you zap us out of here?"

"Yes," Nick said decisively, grabbing Farshad's arm. Nothing happened. "No. We should probably run."

They took off. "If we see the Company Kids we should run the other way," Nick wheezed as he struggled to keep up with Farshad. "They tried to kill us before."

"Roger that," Farshad said. They ducked behind a hedge about a block away from the accident and watched as the ambulance approached. "Do you think they saw us?" he asked.

"Probably not?" Nick whispered, adjusting his glasses. The Hammer was coming to and twisting around with a bewildered look on his face. Nick realized in horror that Rihanna was standing on Ms. Zelle. He gasped. "We left Rihanna! We have to get her!"

He tried to get up but Farshad grabbed him and pulled him back. "Nick. We cannot go back for the chicken."

"Bok!" Rihanna said to the paramedic, who did not seem to know what to do with her.

"But we can't just leave her there!" Nick said. He knew that he sounded like a crazy person, but he didn't care.

"She'll be fine," Farshad hissed, "but we won't be if Ms. Zelle sees us. We need to go. NOW."

Nick had to admit that Farshad was right.

And they were gone.

VERY ROAD INTO MUELLERSVILLE SEEMED TO BE blocked off by parked police cars with flashing red and blue lights, and every time Abe tried a new route they'd just be blocked by more police barricades (from which he always maintained a healthy distance). It seemed to Cookie that they'd circled the entire town before Abe gave up to pull the buggy over to the side of a darkened country road. He hopped off and poked his head through the window. "I don't know what to do," he admitted. "Every road that I know is stopped."

"Could you park this thing and maybe we could walk into town through the woods?" Cookie asked, eyeing the horse. She really didn't want to walk through the woods at night (or ever), but it seemed like a better option than spending another hour in the bumpy buggy going nowhere.

"I could send her back to the farm," Abe murmured, "but then no one would be there to detach her from the buggy. No, I can't do that."

"Then we'll just get out and walk," Cookie said, opening the buggy door and trying and failing to exit with grace. How those Amish girls could do it in their long skirts without falling over was anybody's guess. Martina shrugged and followed her.

"But you can't!" Abe said. "It's not safe."

"Nothing is ever really safe," Martina observed.

"Thanks, Martina, real helpful. Look," Cookie said to Abe. "I've been chased, threatened, teleported, and I've had to hide inside of a sticky dumpster, and that's all happened over the past few hours, so now all I want in the world is to get home, make up some sort of lie about how I got there, take a shower, and go to bed. That. Is. All. I. Want. It's just a short walk through a slightly terrifying dark forest, which compared to everything else we've been through is sort of no big deal. So we're going." She looked expectantly at Martina.

"Bye, Abe," Martina said, and the two set off for the woods.

"Wait!" Abe said, and ran up to them. "Let me try something first." He ran ahead of them to the edge of the forest and stood silently for a moment.

"Is he peeing?" Cookie whispered to Martina.

"No," she whispered back, smiling. "He's trying to help us get home."

There was a rustling in the woods, and Cookie watched in astonishment as animals began to emerge from the shadows. Squirrels first, then groundhogs. A pair of beavers. A family of deer, complete with an enormous stag. Chipmunks. A skunk. Many bunnies.

All the animals gathered in a semicircle around Abe, who continued to stand silently. After a moment he turned back to Cookie and Martina. "They will make sure you get through the forest safely. I have asked them to protect you until you get to the other side."

Cookie couldn't find her voice. She'd seen a lot of unbelievable things since the bus accident, but this was almost too much for her to grasp. Martina grabbed her hand.

"Thank you, Abe." She began to walk to the woods, half dragging the gaping Cookie along with her.

It was very dark and there was no discernable path. Cookie activated the flashlight function on her phone and held it out in front of them. Their wildlife escorts were keeping a safe distance, but when Cookie and Martina moved, they moved with them, scrambling through the undergrowth at the edges of the light from Cookie's phone.

Very slowly and very carefully, they made their way through bramble and over gnarled roots and fallen trees. Cookie clung to Martina for dear life with one hand and to her phone with the other. The idea of spending another hour circling the town in Abe's buggy or even sleeping on a bale of hay next to a bunch of chickens in his neighbor's barn began to seem not quite so bad.

Martina suddenly stopped walking and quickly put her free hand over Cookie's phone, blocking out the light. Cookie could hardly see in front of her own face, but she could feel Martina's hand ferociously squeezing hers.

Did you see something? Cookie struggled to make her thought reach Martina's brain.

The animals. They're tense.

Cookie didn't feel like asking how Martina knew that. She'd just come to accept that Martina knew stuff. And a moment later they heard a howl.

Wolf? Cookie asked desperately, despite the fact that she was pretty sure that was no wolf.

And then the rage thoughts were back, those same thoughts that had terrified and dizzied her at the party. She clung to Martina's hand in the dark.

You HAVE to shut them out, Martina thought to her.

Cookie took a deep breath.

She was Daniesha Cookie Parker. She was the only African American girl in her class at Deborah Reed Middle School. She was the most popular girl in the school, and. She. Was. Not. About. To. Be. Taken. Down. By. Some. Crazed. Science. Experiments! SHE WAS COOKIE PARKER.

The howls were getting closer and it was all Cookie could do to maintain control over her brain. Whose stupid idea had it been to go through the woods anyway?

"They're coming!" Martina whispered, and panicking at the sound of her voice Cookie raised her cell phone flashlight without thinking and pointed it in the direction of the sounds of people crashing through the underbrush.

There were three boys. Eric Mathes (or some madman who had taken over Eric's face and body) and two others, and they froze for a moment as Cookie flashed her light at them. The three were panting like dogs, their bodies coiled as if ready to strike, and their eyes . . . the whites of their eyes had turned blood red.

And for a moment, everything in the dark forest was still.

Then they lunged.

Several things happened at once. Cookie backed up, tripping over a small fallen tree and falling backward. Martina grabbed a fallen branch and began swinging it wildly at the three feral boys.

Then the animals attacked.

When she thought about it later Cookie realized that she would have guessed the bigger animals would have led the charge, but it all started with the chipmunks and the squirrels. They attached themselves to the legs of the mad boys, scampering up them until Eric and his friends were flailing and shrieking. Then came the beavers and the groundhogs, running themselves headlong into the boys' shins, causing them to tumble to the ground, screaming all the while. Then the skunk shimmied up to them. Martina grabbed Cookie's hand and yanked her to her feet.

"WE RUN! NOW!" she screamed, pointing to a young

deer that was hightailing it out of the forest. They followed.

The deer seemed to be leading them on some sort of rough-hewn footpath, and Cookie and Martina ran as fast as they could with only the shaking light of the cell phone to keep them from hitting trees and tripping over rocks. Cookie could no longer hear any other thought besides Martina's *RUN! RUN! RUN!*

The deer stopped as the girls tumbled out of the woods onto a quiet cul-de-sac that was illuminated by a street lamp. Martina turned around and fixed her gray eyes on the deer . "Thank you," she gasped, and the deer turned and ran back into the woods.

"Where are we?" she asked Cookie.

Cookie looked around, trying to get her bearings. "I think we're near Nick's aunts' house, where Jay is." She pointed down the street. "It's around the corner."

Behind them the sounds of the Eric and Friends vs. Woodland Creatures battle got louder. "We need to get inside," Martina said. Cookie nodded, and they ran down the block, still clasping hands.

A minute later they were banging on Nick's aunts' front door. Jay answered, wearing an apron that read *I'm Not a Lesbian but My Wife Is* and a very surprised look on his face. Martina dragged Cookie in and they shut the door before Jay could answer any questions, locking the dead bolt and latching the chain lock before quickly shutting off all the lights in the front of the house and closing the curtains that faced the streets. Cookie collapsed on the living room sofa, too worn-out to help.

The house was quiet and warm, and it smelled like cookies. For the first time in hours Cookie felt something close to safe. Martina joined her on the sofa. Neither of them spoke. Jay disappeared into the kitchen and a moment later came out with a plate of cookies.

"I got bored, so I baked something," he said, putting the plate in front of them.

"I didn't know you baked," Martina said, leaning forward to take a cookie. She handed one to Cookie.

"This was my first time. It's surprisingly easy."

Cookie took a tentative bite. The cookie was still warm and sweet and the chocolate chips inside were gooey. Cookie started to cry. Martina put an arm around her.

Jay sat down on the coffee table in front of them. "When you're ready," he said, "tell me everything."

NE MOMENT HE WAS OUTSIDE LOOKING AT THE wreck of the van and the next Farshad was in a bright, warm kitchen. He stumbled and quickly grabbed hold of a counter to steady himself, accidentally shattering one of the countertop tiles with his right thumb.

"Oh man," Nick groaned, "Molly is going to kill me."

"What . . . where . . ."

"I must have transported us to my aunts' house."

"Did . . . did you mean to?"

"I didn't not mean to . . . ?"

"Well, hey now, the gang's all here!" Jay strode into the room, wearing a rainbow-colored apron. "Cookie and Martina are in the other room and they're a little traumatized. How are you fellows holding up? Are you hungry? I made cookies." He started rummaging through the kitchen cabinets. "Nicholas, be a good lad and tell me where your aunts keep their drinking glasses, I'm all turned around."

"You made cookies in my aunts' kitchen?" Nick asked.

"I was bored. But things are getting interesting now. Look, I found juice boxes in the fridge, your aunts live like they're eight. Bless them. Come, I'm sure the girls will be happy to see you. Or, at least, not totally miserable."

Farshad followed Jay and Nick into the living room, where Cookie and Martina were sitting on the sofa. Both had dirt on their faces and clothes, and it was pretty clear that Cookie had been recently crying. Martina's hands were scratched up and Cookie had leaves in her hair. They looked exhausted.

"You guys look terrible," Nick said, plopping down next to them on the sofa. Farshad was still feeling discombobulated from the trip over and didn't quite know where to put himself.

"Now, now, Nick, while it may be true that the ladies have had harrowing experiences it doesn't mean they're not still very beautiful." Cookie rolled her eyes and Farshad found himself relieved to see her acting like her old Cookie self; seeing her so frail was unnerving. He sat down next to her on the floor and Jay shoved a warm cookie into his hand. It was surprisingly delicious. Farshad could feel his frayed nerves settling down, if ever so slightly.

"Where's Rihanna?" Martina asked Nick.

Nick glowered.

"He'd rather not talk about that," Farshad offered.

"Oh my god, did you guys kill the chicken?" Cookie asked.

"No!" Nick said. "But we kind of had to leave her at an accident scene that we ran away from."

"You were in another accident?" Jay asked, concerned. "With a chicken?"

"No, no, we weren't in the accident . . ."

The stories began to unfold. Nick's teleportation practice with Abe, the Rajavis' reaction to Willis's calculations, the party, Rihanna, the mob, the dumpster, those jerks at the ice cream parlor, The Hammer, the Auxano vans, the accident, Dr. Deery and Ms. Zelle, the mad dash through the woods, Eric's attack, the small army of protective animals, and Jay's newfound baking skills. Farshad, Nick, and Cookie did most of the talking while Martina took out her sketchbook, kicked off her shoes, and tucked her feet under her as she calmly sketched out scenes from the night.

"So are Eric and the others still out there in the woods?" Nick asked.

"Who knows?" Cookie said. "I mean, I don't think the squirrels and chipmunks were trying to kill them. They were just trying to stop them."

"I don't think squirrels eat people," Martina agreed.

"Who cares if they get eaten by squirrels?" Farshad snapped, and immediately regretted it. Eric and his friends might be jerks but they were clearly not okay and getting eaten by squirrels was not the answer. "Sorry," he muttered.

"What's going to happen to all the other Company Kids who didn't get out?" Cookie asked. "The ones that were in the six other vans?"

"Who cares?" Farshad asked bitterly. They had just tried to kill him.

"I care. They're my friends."

"Some friends."

"It's not their fault that they've gone . . . feral."

"You seem to be forgetting that they weren't particularly swell before they became a violent mob."

"Look, I know you don't like them and they've been really mean to you—I was really mean to you—but they're just kids and they're in trouble and we can't just let them get trapped in that lab without doing anything about it. We have to help them."

"They probably are helping them!" Farshad exploded. "That's why they probably grabbed them in the first place, so they couldn't hurt themselves or each other!"

"Just like they helped Mr. Friend?" Martina asked.

Everyone fell silent.

Farshad threw his hands in the air. "So, what are we supposed to do?" He looked around the group. Jay started to lean forward. "Oh no no no"—Farshad stopped him—"the last time I followed one of your suggestions I ended up getting hunted by a bloodthirsty mob and got stuck in a minivan with a shrieking weirdo who knew nothing and was no help at all. No more Jay Plans!"

"Wait, wait," Jay said. "I don't have any Jay Plans. Is that a thing now? Because I LOVE IT." Farshad glared at Jay, who raised his palms up. "Wait! I don't have a plan. But I have a thought. You know what we haven't talked about yet?"

"How our parents are probably frantically worried about us?" Farshad snarled.

"Perhaps, but no, I was thinking about Willis's calculations," Jay said. "You said that your parents were very disturbed by them. What exactly did they say?"

Farshad tried to remember. It seemed like it had been a month since he had last seen his parents. "They said that it was similar to something they'd been working on at Auxano," he murmured.

"Right. And what do you think that might be?"

"How should I know?"

"What is the most important thing that Auxano is working on right now?" Jay asked. He had begun to pace the room with a wild look in his eyes. "Something that they've spent a lot of time and money on. Something RISKY. Something so important that they're willing to shut down an entire town just to keep it under wraps!"

"The formula that made us this way," Martina whispered.

"Do you think those calculations are related to Dr. Deery's formula?" Nick asked, his mouth agape.

"Oh, I have no idea," Jay said, sitting down. "It looked like utter gobbledygook to me. But I know who would know." He leaned forward. "We need to talk to Willis."

Cookie let out a snort-laugh. "You're kidding me, right?" she asked. "Dude can't talk."

"No, no, my dearest friend who I very much respect, it's not that he can't talk. It's that he *won't* talk. We need to find a way to talk to him."

"That's madness. We can't even leave this house," Farshad said, looking at the curtained windows.

"Yes, we can," Martina said, looking at Nick.

Nick stared at her, his eyes as round as saucers. "What, I'm supposed to transport everyone to Rebecca and Beanie's apartment now? What makes you think I can do that?"

"Because you can," said Martina.

"Easy for you to say," Nick grumbled, looking at his scuffed-up sneakers.

"Just try."

"Why?" Nick said. "Haven't we done enough?"

Farshad looked at Nick. He looked lost, and despite his frustration, Farshad felt very, deeply sorry for him. All Nick ever wanted was to help people, but he didn't have the faith in his own abilities to do so. That's why he always hung around Jay—if there's one thing Jay was really, really good at, it was the one thing that Nick was really, really bad at: believing that he could do or be anything, even if that thing was completely ridiculous. A guy like Nick needed a guy like Jay to show him that anything is possible. And a guy like Jay needed a guy like Nick around to keep him from trying to use suction cups to scale the Auxano building or eat a whole tire or whatever bananas idea Jay came up with next.

These are my friends now, Farshad realized. *I finally have friends, and they are really, really odd.*

And where did he fit in?

"I think you can do it," Farshad heard himself saying. He shot a quick look to Cookie, who looked just as surprised to hear him say it as he was; she was definitely not at the steering wheel of his brain. But something inside him knew that Nick needed to try to help, and if he gave up, he'd be worse off, because the world needed more people like Nick: people who did the right thing just because it was the right thing to do.

Thinking too hard about helping the jerks who had made Farshad's life miserable for years was beginning to hurt his head, but he kept talking. "Look, we've got these powers, and they're all getting stronger." He shot a quick glance to Martina, the only one in their group whose power didn't seem like much of anything, but he kept going. "And you were right," he said to Nick. "If we don't harness them and use them, then we don't deserve them. It feels wrong to just sit on our abilities while kids we know are being rounded up and used as lab rats."

"So you expect me to be able to somehow zap all of us to

Rebecca and Beanie's apartment?" Nick asked with a helpless gesture that clearly said, *Are you kidding me?*

"Yes," Martina said, at the same time as Cookie said, "You could try," and Jay said, "Maybe have another cookie first."

"Okay," Nick said, pacing, "okay okay okay. Maybe we should all prepare. You know. Go to the bathroom first? Maybe? Do we need to pack anything? Maybe we should bring—"

Martina leapt up from the sofa, grabbed Nick's arm, and yelled, "GO TO WILLIS NOW!"

And they disappeared.

Farshad, Cookie, and Jay were silent for a moment. "Maybe I should pack some cookies for when Nick comes back to get us," Jay said.

"Make sure you've turned off the oven," Cookie murmured as Jay scampered back into the kitchen in search of sandwich bags.

"Do you think they actually made it to Rebecca and Beanie's apartment?" Farshad asked.

Cookie sank back into the sofa. "The next time we're going on one of these adventures," she growled, "everyone's getting a frigging cell phone."

**N**ICK FLOPPED ONTO REBECCA AND BEANIE'S WORN-out couch and closed his eyes. He'd done it, and he didn't exactly know how to feel about what he'd done. He'd purposefully transported both himself and another person all the way to Lancaster, to a specific place.

What did this mean? Could he go anywhere? If he thought too hard about Hawaii, would he just end up in Hawaii? Could he take his mom on the Hawaiian vacation she'd always wanted? But what if they got stuck in Hawaii? HE HAD TO STOP THINKING ABOUT HAWAII. Nick opened his eyes. He was not in Hawaii.

"You took my notes," Willis said. He was crouched on the sofa next to Nick, his eyes wild. "You took them."

"Yes," Nick said, "I did. I'm sorry."

"You took my notes."

"This is all he's been talking about since you left last time," Rebecca said wearily. She walked over to the sofa and reached out to Willis, who recoiled and tried to hide underneath the cushions. "But at least he's been talking."

"Of course I can talk," Willis said, his voice muffled behind a pillow. "Of course of course of course and he took my notes and I need those notes."

"What do you need the notes for?" Martina asked. She sat on the sofa between Nick and the pile of cushions that wasn't doing a particularly good job of hiding Willis.

"I need them because I need them. I do. I need them. And he took them. And he needs to give them back because I need them."

Martina looked at Nick. "Can you get them back?"

Nick looked at Willis, who was chewing furiously on the cuticle of his left thumb. He felt helpless. "I don't even know where they are." He looked over Martina at Willis. "I'm really, really sorry. I didn't realize how important they were."

"They are very important! Super important! They are of the utmost importance!" Willis cried.

"But why, Willis?" Rebecca asked gently.

"Because! Because they are! Because I can use them to stop . . . all . . . of . . . this!"

"All of what?" Nick asked.

"Our powers," Martina said.

"What?" Rebecca asked. "Willis, are you serious?"

"WHY WOULD I BE JOKING?" Willis screamed, and began throwing pillows at Rebecca. "I. CAN. MAKE. THIS. STOP."

Rebecca dodged the cushions. "You can make us normal again?" she asked when he was out of ammunition.

"OF COURSE I CAN WHY WILL NO ONE UNDERSTAND ME?" he shrieked.

"I understand," Martina said. Nick stared at her, wondering again what her power was. Maybe it was understanding people like Willis. And seeing vortexes. And invisible men.

"I need those notes back," Willis told her, beginning to cry. He looked small and frail as the sobs shook his body. "I *need* them."

"I'm so sorry . . ." Nick whispered.

"If he has his notes, we will all be normal again?" Rebecca interrupted, hopeful.

"What is going on?" Beanie asked. He had just come into the apartment with an armful of groceries and was surveying the situation. "Did the sofa explode? Oh, hello Nick."

"Willis has been working on a way to make us normal again," Rebecca said, her voice shaking.

"IT IS A CHEMICAL FORMULA THAT WOULD NEGATE THE EFFECTS OF THE FIRST FORMULA!" Willis screamed, and went back to crying.

"We need it," Nick said, trying not to sound scared. "Ms. Zelle and the people at Auxano have been giving it to our classmates and it's made them act like wild animals. We need it to stop them."

"Oh," Beanie said, putting down the groceries. He picked a knitted blanket off the floor and wrapped it around Willis, and then grabbed one of the notebooks and a pencil to give to him. Willis immediately stopped crying and started scribbling, once again oblivious to everyone else in the room.

"We have to help them," Rebecca said, and gestured to Willis. "We have to help him."

Beanie frowned. "Would we lose our powers as well?"

"Of course!" Rebecca cried. "And then we will all be normal again."

Beanie leaned against a wall and looked at his feet. "I do not know if I want to be normal again."

"What?"

"Rebecca—"

"No! We talked about this!" Rebecca paced the apartment, agitated. "If we were normal the Auxano people would stop coming after us. We would not have to hide anymore. We could go home. Beanie, HOME. I want to go home!"

"We do not even know if we would be welcomed back home," Beanie said, still looking at the floor. "And *we* did not talk about this. *You* talked about it." He glanced over at Willis. "He needs help, yes. But I do not know if I need help."

"But if you are not normal you will certainly not be able to come back. With me. I thought you wanted to come back with me." Rebecca seemed on the verge of tears and Nick felt a sudden desire to be anywhere but in that apartment witnessing something that seemed like not at all his business.

And then Nick was in a long hallway with no windows. He'd been in this hallway before . . .

He was at Auxano, in the hallway where they'd found the earsplittingly-loud screaming bunnies. *GET OUT OF HERE!* Nick mentally shouted to himself. But he stayed put.

He heard footsteps and voices, and looked frantically around for a hiding place. The door nearest to him was locked, as was the next one down the hall. The third door was open, but it was a women's bathroom. Nick could hear the footsteps getting closer. He held his breath and slipped into the restroom.

It looked just like a men's room, only there were more stalls and no urinals, with a small basket full of markers wrapped in white plastic. On closer inspection, those were definitely not markers. Nick heard the voices coming closer, and saw that the bathroom door was opening. He quickly ducked into a stall and locked it, hoping that the women coming in wouldn't notice his beat-up gray sneakers.

"Ugh, I had to get out of there," one woman was saying as she entered the stall next to Nick's. "Maggie swore they were getting better, but I don't see it. Four of them had to be separated for biting and we had to put an actual muzzle on that Izaak kid."

"And where is Maggie, anyway?" The other woman got into the stall on the other side of Nick. "She should be here."

"I don't know." The woman sighed. "This whole thing is a nightmare. Do you think they're ever going to let us go home?"

The women reminded Nick of his mom and his aunts, who would also have uninterrupted conversations while one of them was in the bathroom. Women were weird.

"Dr. Carpenter keeps telling me that it won't be long, but I'm pretty sure he has no idea what he's talking about."

"Dr. Carpenter definitely knows what's going on."

"Oh, the other Dr. Carpenter, sure. Her husband is in a panic, though."

"Aren't we all."

Dr. Carpenter and Dr. Carpenter? Jay's parents? Nick let out a little gasp.

The women stopped talking. Had they heard him? They had definitely heard him. They knew he had been listening. Nick thought fast and shoved his hand through the neck of his T-shirt into his armpit and brought his arm down, making a fairly realistic farting sound. Then he did it again. And again. And again.

The women quickly finished their bathroom business and headed out the door. "Oh my god . . ." he heard one of them saying as the bathroom door closed. Nick let out a sigh of relief and removed his clammy hand from his armpit. Jay was going to get a kick out of this, if he ever saw Jay again.

"Old sport, where have you been?" Jay asked. Nick was back in his aunts' living room.

But how was he going to tell Jay that his parents knew . . . everything?

COOKIE DIDN'T KNOW IF SHE WAS GETTING USED TO Nick popping in and out of thin air or if she was just really tired and didn't care. This was her new normal! Hanging out with her weirdo friends who had magical powers that they couldn't control while their entire town was on lockdown. No biggie.

She texted her mom and lied, yet again, telling her that she was still at the party and that everything was fine. The boys were playing video games and the girls were painting their nails different colors (more details now, fewer questions later). She put away her phone as Nick told them about his unintended trip to Auxano.

"So they're not getting any better," Jay said, pacing furiously, "and the Auxano people don't know how to make them better. But Willis does."

"Willis did," Nick explained, "and he wrote it down, and we need his notes." He looked at Farshad. "Can you get them back from your parents?"

Farshad rubbed his temples. "I don't know where they put them. It seemed like they knew what they were—they probably took them to Auxano already."

"Wait, did you just abandon Martina at Rebecca and Beanie's apartment?" Cookie asked.

"Uh . . ." Nick looked at his shoes. "I guess I kinda did?"

"Nick!"

"Teleporting is tricky! I don't know what I'm doing!"

"Martina is probably fine," Jay said. "She's a very resourceful young woman and Rebecca and Beanie have always been gracious hosts. I assume," he said, most likely remembering that he'd never actually met them. "The real question is, are we certain that your parents know what to do with Willis's calculations?"

Farshad threw his hands up in the air. "Do *we* know

what to do with Willis's calculations?" He looked at Jay. "We can't trust Dr. Deery with them. We certainly can't trust Ms. Zelle. How would we know that Auxano even wants to make everyone better? They might just want to make them stronger!"

"Maybe my parents would know what to do," Jay mused.

"No!" Nick blurted, and immediately looked uncomfortable.

Cookie perked up. She had always been good at reading people, but it didn't take a mind reader to tell that Nick was hiding something.

"I know they can be a little standoffish, but they might prove resourceful," Jay said, oblivious to Nick's squirming.

What do you know about Jay's parents? Cookie aimed her thoughts at Nick.

"Nothing!" Nick said.

"Nothing what?" Jay asked.

"We need a plan," Farshad said decisively. "One that helps the kids and Invisible Ed and Mr. Friend, if he's still around."

"Okay," Jay said, still pacing. "Let's figure something out . . ."

"I'm going to put these cookies away before I eat them all and there's none left for Nick's aunts," Cookie declared, gathering the platter. "Show me where your aunts keep the cookie tin?" she asked Nick, giving him a hard stare. He followed her into the kitchen.

"You're keeping something from Jay about his parents!" she hissed to Nick the moment they got into the kitchen.

"No, I'm not!" Nick said, turning red in the face.

Cookie grabbed his arm. "Don't you dare go—"

They were in a barn.

"—teleporting anywhere. Are you kidding me?!?"

"I didn't mean to!" Nick said. "I got flustered!"

"Where are we?"

"Hi, Nick. Hello, Cookie." Abe was in the corner of the barn, putting his horse back into a stall. "Nice to see you both again. Why are you here?"

"Nick didn't want to answer a question so he freaked out and teleported us here!" Cookie growled.

"Oh."

"Jay's parents already know about the formula!" Nick said. "I overheard two scientists talking about them while I was hiding in the women's bathroom! They know everything! They're part of the whole experiment! I think his mother might be in charge of the whole thing!"

"Oh no," Cookie gasped.

"Why were you hiding in a women's bathroom?" Abe asked.

"I can't tell him!" Nick said. "He's already worried that his parents manufactured his intelligence and if he finds out that they're part of this whole mess he'll never know for sure and it will really hurt him!"

Cookie scoffed. "Of course they didn't manufacture Jay's intelligence. He's not that smart."

"Hey. He does really well at school." Nick seemed offended on behalf of his friend, which Cookie couldn't help but find incredibly sweet. But she was still in a barn miles away from civilization, so that feeling went away pretty quickly.

"Okay, but Jay hasn't turned feral or started melting metal with his laser-beam eyes or anything. If his parents had been able to use the formula to alter him then why would they have messed up so royally on everyone else? It doesn't make sense."

"None of this makes any sense. But we still can't tell him about them. They're his parents."

"He's going to have to know eventually! He probably already suspects something."

"He does! And he was really upset about the idea of it. I don't think he could handle the reality of it."

"Jay can handle a lot more than you give him credit for. I—" Cookie paused for a moment, not wanting to say what she knew she had to say next. "I really hurt him. I mean, really. I showed him stuff about how he made me feel that he wasn't at all prepared to know. You saw it."

Nick nodded.

"And you know what? He bounced back. Because he's Jay. And that's what Jay does. He can handle it. You don't have to always protect him."

"So . . . what's going on?" Abe asked.

"This is sort of a private conversation, Abe," Cookie snapped.

"My apologies. It is my neighbor's barn, though."

"Sorry, Abe," Nick said.

"Yeah, I'm sorry," Cookie said, feeling bad. "And I never got to thank you for sending those animals to protect us. It was very thoughtful. And freaky. And kind of life-saving."

"I was happy to be able to help. So were the animals. They liked you."

"Really? You could tell that?"

"They wouldn't have helped if they didn't want to."

"Oh." Suddenly Cookie had an idea. It wasn't a great idea, but it was an idea. "Nick. Nick, you have to get us back to the others. I think I have a plan."

"Is it a good plan?" Nick asked.

"No," said Cookie, "but it is a plan." She grabbed his hand. "TAKE US BACK TO YOUR AUNTS' HOUSE!"

"Why are you yelling at me?"

"I don't know, it worked before when Martina did it?"

"She startled me. I kind of expect you to yell at me."

"Hey!"

"What? I do!"

"Well, let's get back. And bring Abe with us." Cookie looked at Abe. "We need your help. Are you up for it?"

Abe nodded and Nick took hold of his hand. Nothing happened.

"What are we doing?" Abe asked after a while.

"I'm trying to teleport us all back to my aunts' house."

"Have you . . . teleported . . . more than one other person before?"

"Sure," Cookie said, "he brought me and Martina here when we were trapped in the dumpster."

"And Rihanna," Nick said ruefully.

"Ah, right," Abe said. "So how were you feeling when that happened?"

"Terrified! And I just really wanted to be anywhere else other than there."

"So we should make you terrified." Abe thought. "GRRRR I AM A HORRIBLE BEAR!"

"Dude."

"GRRRRR I AM A BEAR WITH A KNIFE."

"I think we need to try something else."

"BUT WAIT MY KNIFE IS VERY SHARP, GRRRR."

"This is amazing. Can I film this?" Cookie asked.

"Why?" Abe asked.

"Everyone, please be quiet, let me clear my head," Nick said, feeling the pressure of Cookie's and Abe's hands in his. He closed his eyes and thought about the warmth and safety of his aunts' house; about Jay; about Jay's parents . . .

"Where are we?" Cookie asked, looking around what seemed to be the living room of a sparsely decorated sub-urban house. In the corner of a sofa sat a balding man with glasses who was staring at a coffee table full of papers. The man looked up, understandably shocked to see them.

"Nick?" he asked.

NICK BLINKED. THEY WERE STANDING IN JAY'S LIVING room. They were standing in Jay's living room and Jay's dad had been staring at Willis's notes.

"Oh hey, Dr. Carpenter," Nick said, weakly trying to make it seem normal that he was suddenly in the man's living room holding hands with an African American girl and an Amish teenager. Doo dee doo, nothing to see here.

Jay's dad blinked a few times. "Well . . . hello, Nick, old boy," he said carefully. "How . . . how did you get here?"

"Where are we?" Abe asked, looking around nervously at the Carpenters' living room.

"This is Jay's dad," Nick said, trying to sound calm and like a totally normal person in a not-at-all-bonkers situation. "And Jay's house."

"It looks so normal," Cookie said.

"So . . . hello," Jay's father said again, putting down the papers. It was clearly Willis's work. "Nicholas, I would like an answer to my question, please."

We have to get those papers, Nick thought wildly to Cookie, and out of the corner of his eye he saw her give a slight, almost imperceptible nod.

"Oh . . . we were just looking for Jay," Nick said.

"Jay's in his room," Dr. Carpenter said. "Studying. Because there's a curfew and no one should be out and about right now. Did you . . . did you come in through the garage?"

"If he's studying, we'll just leave him alone," Nick said. "I always forget that Jay studies, because school just seems to come so easily to him." Cookie gave his hand a squeeze. She was going to go for the papers.

"You can't go anywhere, Nick, you should never have been out in the first place . . . Does your mother know you're here? And who are these two—"

Cookie leapt forward, grabbed all of Willis's notes, and screamed, "GOT THEM! GO! GO!" as she flung herself into Nick's arms, and a second later they were back in Jilly and Molly's living room.

"We did it!" Nick exclaimed.

"Where's Abe?" Cookie gasped.

"GAH!" Nick said, teleporting once more to Jay's living room to find Abe standing awkwardly in front of Dr. Carpenter, who was just screaming.

"Sorry sorry sorry!" Nick yelped, grabbing Abe, and a half-second later they were standing in Rebecca and Beanie's living room.

"AAAAUUGH!" Beanie screamed.

"Hi, guys," Martina said. She was curled up in a corner of the old plaid sofa, drawing what looked like a picture of Cookie hugging Nick. Nick figured it was better not to ask.

"Abe!" Rebecca ran to her brother and gave him a hug.

"Where are my notes?" Willis growled from his spot

on the floor next to the sofa. "I need my notes. I NEED THEM."

"We got them!" Nick exclaimed, happy to give good news for once. "Well, Cookie has them. But they're definitely had."

Willis looked at him blankly.

"We have them. We just don't have them here," Nick explained. "I'm not sure how exactly I got us here."

"I need them HERE. With me," Willis said.

"Well, yes, we are working on that." Nick felt deeply uncomfortable as Willis stared at him without blinking. He cleared his throat.

"When you have them, will you be able to . . . fix things?"

"Yes, yes, of course, of course, that's why I need them," Willis muttered. "So we can go back to being like we were before and not being like this, yes, yes, yes."

"What would you need, besides the papers?" Nick asked gently.

"A CENTRIFUGE, OF COURSE," Willis snapped, and then quieted down. "And an enclosed room, yes, and a sample of the original formula."

"And you're sure this will work?"

"OF COURSE I AM SURE." Willis bent back over his notebook. "Of course of course of course."

Nick looked at Martina, who gave him a little shrug. Of course.

**F**ARSHAD, COOKIE, AND JAY LOOKED OVER THE papers that Nick had retrieved. "Do you really think this will help us?" he murmured, completely unable to comprehend any of Willis's equations.

"Oh, ye of little faith," Jay said, taking off his ridiculous apron and tossing it over the back of a chair. "Of course it will help the Company Kids."

"And you guys were able to grab these from my parents' house without them noticing?" Farshad asked Cookie.

Cookie gave him A Look.

Don't ask where we found the papers.

Farshad sighed. He didn't have the time or energy for this sort of thing. "Why."

"Hmm?" Jay asked, looking up.

I'll tell you later. Cookie shot a quick, almost imperceptible glance toward Jay. There was something she didn't want him to hear. "Where is Nick?" she asked, starting to pace around the living room.

"Here!" Nick said, reappearing next to Jay and flopping on the sofa. "I've just been to Rebecca and Beanie's place."

"Did you get Abe?" Cookie asked, worried.

"Yes, he's fine, he's there, and Willis is sure that if we

get his papers back to him we can cure the Company Kids. And Mr. Friend and Invisible Ed, if we can find them. And possibly ourselves."

"What do you mean, possibly ourselves?" Jay asked.

"Willis thinks he can make some sort of antidote spray that will neutralize the effects of Dr. Deery's formula," Nick said. "He says that if we're able to spray the Company Kids, they'll go back to being their dumb old selves."

"I'm all for that," Farshad said.

"But what if you inhale the spray?" Jay asked.

"Then we're neutralized, too," Nick said, "and everything goes back to normal, I guess."

Farshad looked at his hands. Going back to normal meant his super strength would be gone. On one hand, no more crushed devices and broken countertops. On the other, he'd never again be able to use his power to be a superhero.

But he didn't want to be a superhero. He didn't. All he had ever wanted was to get through school and leave Muellersville and never come back.

"If that's what it takes, I'm okay with it," he said.

"I'm not!" Jay stood up and stomped his foot for emphasis. "I am emphatically not okay with you guys losing your powers." Stamp, stamp, stamp.

"Well, it isn't really up to you," Farshad told him, annoyed.

"Nick," Jay implored, turning away from Farshad, "you are starting to be able to zap yourself wherever you want to go. And now you can bring people with you! You can bring your mom to Hawaii! Why would you willingly part with that?"

Nick looked helpless. "Once the spray is in the air we're going to be breathing it in," he said. "I don't know how we can spray it without being affected by it."

"I'll do it!" Jay yelped. "I'll distribute the spray! It won't affect me, I don't have any powers."

Nick looked stricken. "But maybe you do," he said.

"What do you mean? Of course I don't, we've established that," Jay said. He turned to Cookie. "Do you want to lose your ability to communicate with your mind? You're just starting to get the hang of it!"

Cookie looked down. "You don't know what it's like," she said softly, and Farshad couldn't help but feel for her. "Ninety percent of the time I don't want to hear what people are thinking. Especially if they're thinking things about me."

"But you're learning to control it," Jay said. "Just give it a little time. Can you even imagine the potential of what you could learn and do?"

Cookie sighed. "If losing my power is what it takes to get my friends back, then I'm okay with it."

Jay threw his hands up in the air. "But you don't have to! I can do it! Nick can zap me into Auxano, we can find the Company Kids, he can zap out, I can spray them in the face, easy peasy lemon squeezy!"

"That doesn't actually sound that easy," Farshad observed.

"You can't do it!" Nick cried.

"Then I'll get help," Jay said with a wave of his hand.

"From who?" Farshad asked, exasperated. "We have no one on our side. The Auxano people just want their formula to work and are clearly willing to use their own children as guinea pigs and then kidnap them. Dr. Deery is in deep with Ms. Zelle, and half our parents work for Auxano and haven't done anything to stop it because Auxano controls the whole town. They shut it down, for godssake! No one is going to back us up."

"And I don't think it's a great idea for you to do it at all," Nick said.

"I'm ignoring you, it is a great idea. All you and the others have to do is get us in, and we will do the rest."

"Who's we?" Farshad asked.

Jay turned to him, his eyes twinkling. "An old friend who owes us a favor."

I **T HAD TAKEN NICK AND JAY FOUR TRIES TO GET CLOSE TO** Kaylee Schmitt's house (they'd first ended up back in Abe's neighbor's barn, then Nick's old house, and then at the Understeps in the darkened school) before finally getting close enough to the Schmitt farm, less than a mile away from the Auxano campus, to walk up to the house at nine in the evening. Nick stopped before they reached the front door.

"I don't know about this," he said, staying in the shadows outside of the range of the light on the front porch of the house.

"Nicholas. Come on, you stalwart old lemur, there's nothing not to know," Jay said, although he, too, remained in the shadows.

"You're really reaching new heights of nonsense-talk," Nick said, looking at the front door. Kaylee had four older brothers and they were all enormous. Nick wasn't scared of them, per se, but he also didn't particularly want them to know he existed. Rumor had it that they'd once filled the high school boys' locker room with goats from their farm.

"It's been a bit of a challenging day," Jay admitted. "But, come on. We're here, we've finally made it—"

"I was trying!"

"And you were doing a marvelous job, and now we're here. We might as well get what we came for."

"What *you* came for. No one else was particularly in love with this plan."

"Yes, true, but no one was vehemently against it, either."

"Farshad specifically said that it could possibly be your worst idea yet."

"Well, the night is still young and our man Farshad is entirely too negative. When this is all over we should take him to Dutch Wonderland or something." Jay threw back his narrow shoulders. "Let's do this."

Nick followed his friend to the door, and after a moment of knocking one of Kaylee's brothers was looking at the two twelve-year-olds on his front porch with undisguised curiosity.

"Hello!" Jay blurted to the gigantic teenager. "Pardon the lateness of the hour, but is Kaylee available?"

"Uh . . . yeah," the teenager said. "KAYL. GET DOWN HERE. SOME NERD WANTS TO SEE YOU."

"WHO?" Kaylee Schmitt's voice called from up the stairs.

"I DON'T KNOW, SOME NERD."

"Jay Carpenter," Jay helpfully interjected.

"JAY CARPETER."

"Carpenter, my dear man, it's not that difficult."

"SOME NERD." They could hear Kaylee coming down the stairs. "She's coming," the brother said.

"Yes, thank you so much," Jay said, and Nick could tell that Kaylee's brother was trying to figure out whether or not Jay was being a punk to him. Nick was used to people wondering that about his best friend.

Kaylee looked first surprised and then suspicious to see them. "Uh, hi," she said, making no moves to invite them into the house. She looked around, and definitely seemed confused. The Schmitts' house was very far back from the main road, and two kids without a car or bikes would have had to walk a very long way to get there. The Schmitts didn't get a lot of drop-in visitors. "What's up?"

"Kaylee," Jay said happily, "how nice to see you. How are you faring after our little encounter today?"

"I'm fine," she said warily as her towering brother looked on with curiosity. "What are you doing here?"

"Do you mind if we come in and sit down?" Jay asked. "We have a story to tell you."

When Jay was done talking Kaylee and her four brothers sat in silence. They were all sitting on a long L-shaped sofa; first Kaylee, then Kyle, Kurt, Kameron, and Korbin. Their mother was working a late shift at the call center and their father was already asleep, so Jay told the story of the bus accident and everything that had happened since in an uncharacteristically hushed tone while the Schmitt siblings listened attentively. Nick noticed that they had been shooting one another looks while Jay talked. After a moment, Kyle turned to Kaylee.

"Text Paul. Tell him to come over and bring the goat."

Nick looked at Jay, who seemed equally confused as Kaylee hunched over her cell phone, texting furiously. "Goat?" Nick asked tentatively.

"Yeah," Kyle said. "Goat." He thought a moment before speaking again. "So, nothing you've told us just now is that surprising."

"I'm surprised about Ms. Zelle being involved." Kurt sighed. "I liked her."

Kyle rolled his eyes. "What I'm saying is that the people who don't live in town have known for a while that messed-up stuff was happening at Auxano."

"Why haven't you told anyone?" Nick asked.

Korbin snorted. "Who's going to believe us?"

"But what did you mean by 'messed-up stuff'?" Jay asked.

"Paul is on his way," Kaylee said. "You'll see."

A few minutes later they were all standing on the front porch as Paul Yoder approached, coaxing a goat to come along with him. "Come on," he grumbled, "we're almost there."

"Want food," the goat said.

"You just ate," Paul said.

"Want more food," the goat replied.

"Did I just hear that goat talk?" Jay asked, incredulous.

"Yeah," Paul said. "Hey, Jay. Hey, Jay's friend."

"Want more food now," the goat said.

"Holy smacks," Nick breathed.

"Do you have food? Want food."

"This is extraordinary," Jay whispered.

"Not really. All she ever does is ask for more food," Paul said.

"About a month ago Gertie over there wandered off," Kaylee explained, "and Paul found that she'd broken into the Auxano campus and was eating their garbage, and she's been talking ever since."

"Name not Gertie. Name MAAAAAAAHH. Want more food."

"Should I get her something?" Kaylee asked Paul.

"Not if you think it's going to stop her from asking for more," Paul growled.

"This is incredible." Jay was excited. "Did you tell Auxano about it?"

"No!" Kyle snapped. "We don't tell them anything. They've been trying for years to buy out our farms so they can do their creepy experiments. You can't trust anything they do or say. Look at what they did to Gertie!"

"MAAAAAAAHH. Feed me."

"So if what Kaylee texted me is true," Paul said, "could you cure Gertie and make her less annoying?"

"*You're* annoying. Feed me."

"Yes," Jay said. "But we need help."

COOKIE
Can manipulate people into letting us into restricted areas (that are not just the women's bathroom).
ABE
Will stay outside as emergency backup.
Maker of the antidote
WILLIS
REBECCA
Protecting Willis
BEANIE

THE PLAN WAS SIMPLE. NICK WOULD TELEPORT everyone except for the Farm Kids to the women's bathroom at Auxano (he'd done several test runs, and every time had ended up in the women's bathroom). Then Rebecca, Beanie, Cookie, and Jay would escort Willis to the lab with the enormous centrifuge while Farshad, Martina, and Nick found the Company Kids, Mr. Friend, and Invisible Ed. Then they'd all meet up and Jay would spray everyone. The Farm Kids would storm the facilities to cause mayhem and get them out, as once the spray was in the air anyone present with powers would be normal again. The Company Kids would be cured, along with Rebecca and Beanie and whomever else wanted to stay to get sprayed, and they'd all get out of there and continue on with their lives.

Simple.

Cookie looked around the room again. Everyone except for Martina and Willis looked anxious, and she could hear and feel the nervous thoughts swirling around her. Kaylee, Paul, and the rest of the Farm Kids were freaked out. Cookie couldn't blame them—they'd just seen Nick teleport for the first time (although they had opted to drive to Rebecca and Beanie's in Kyle's truck). Korbin in particular was staring at Martina, trying to catch her eyes changing color. He should have been more worried about Cookie hearing his thoughts, but people tend to pay more attention to the wonders they're able to see (even though Martina was looking down at her sketchbook, as usual).

It was difficult enough for Cookie to gather her own thoughts without the jumble of Farm Kid anxiety creeping at the edges of her brain. She rubbed her temples.

Let's go outside.

Cookie looked up and saw that Martina had planted a thought in her brain. She was too good at that, although Cookie didn't really mind. Martina only sent thoughts to her when it was necessary, and like Martina herself they weren't that intrusive. She stood up. "I need some fresh air," she declared.

Nick shot her a concerned look.

"Don't worry, I'm fine, I just need to get my head in order before we do this thing," Cookie said, and headed out the door of the apartment. Martina followed, and Cookie was pretty sure that no one (besides Korbin) even noticed.

They walked silently down the stairs of the old house where Rebecca and Beanie lived to the driveway, where Kyle's truck was parked. Cookie leaned against it. Martina looked at her. She didn't even have to ask what Cookie was thinking and Cookie knew it.

"I don't know what I'm going to do," Cookie said.

Martina looked at her questioningly, her gray eyes turning a light blue.

"What?"

"I didn't say anything."

"You didn't need to, your eyes are all changing color."

"I don't know why they do that."

"Oh, I'm pretty sure they correspond with your thoughts," Cookie said. "I just haven't figured out the pattern yet. Do they turn blue when you're happy and green when you're scared and purple when you're hungry?"

"Are they purple now?"

"Wait, are you hungry?"

"Kind of."

"I was just saying. They're still blue. I don't actually think I've seen them turn full purple." Cookie took a deep breath. "Do you know what you're going to do?"

Martina looked up at the night sky. "I think I'm going to stay the way I am," Martina said. "If I can."

"Well it's easy for you," Cookie grumbled. "Your power isn't driving you up the wall."

"I was probably already up a wall anyway," Martina said.

"Tell me something," Cookie said. "Your power is more than just your eyes changing color, isn't it?"

Martina nodded.

"But it has a lot to do with your eyes," Cookie prompted, looking expectantly at Martina, who looked up at the stars.

"I think I see things that other people don't see," she said quietly.

"Like when you could see Invisible Ed."

"Right. And how I could tell where we were going in the woods without much light. And what I see when I teleport with Nick. Lots of things."

"And you want to keep seeing them," Cookie said. Martina nodded again.

"But why haven't you told us about this before?" Cookie asked.

"I figured you would all just think I'm crazy," Martina said.

Cookie laughed. "That's ridiculous," she said, "we already think you're crazy."

Martina looked at Cookie in surprise, and then let out the loudest laugh Cookie had ever heard. She laughed until she was nearly doubled over with laughter, and Cookie couldn't help but join in.

It felt really, really good to laugh. The girls clutched their sides and leaned on the truck and laughed and laughed, because if they didn't they'd probably start crying (or Cookie would, at least). She couldn't remember the last time she'd laughed as hard or as long as she was laughing, and after a while she couldn't even remember what they were laughing about. She just knew that laughing felt great.

"So," Martina said, once they'd finally quieted down and caught their breath. "Do you want to keep your power?"

"No," Cookie said, and was surprised to hear it coming out

of her mouth. Martina looked at her expectantly and Cookie half wondered if she could see something that Cookie couldn't.

"Look, I'm the only black kid in school. I already know what people are thinking half the time. Do I need to read minds as well?" she asked.

"I suppose not," Martina said, and paused for a moment. "Are you afraid of what you can do?"

Cookie looked up. The stars were incredible, something she was never able to see when she visited Philadelphia. "After what happened with Jay, yes," she whispered.

"That makes sense," Martina said, and it was a relief to hear her say it. Cookie felt strangely lighter.

"You know, I've never had a friend that I didn't feel like I needed to impress before," Cookie admitted.

"I've never had a friend before," Martina responded, and Cookie laughed.

"Well, you do now," she said, linking her arm in Martina's and heading back to the house. "Let's go raid a laboratory and save some deranged chemically altered middle schoolers. It's what friends do."

"Friendship is weird."

"Sure is."

FARSHAD STOOD WITH THE STRANGE GROUP OF NEW friends and nervous allies at the edge of the forest near the east wing of the Auxano campus. In the distance he was able to see the same door that they'd escaped from during their last raid on the chemical company. The doorknob that he'd crushed with his thumbs had been replaced, and for a moment he wondered if they'd taken his thumbprint. It was probably better not to think about it. But now he kind of wished he was wearing gloves.

In the Schmitts' trunk on the way over Cookie had announced that she would be taking the antidote and giving up her powers. Farshad had expected Jay to try to dissuade her, but Jay had just given Cookie a quick nod; something about his encounter with her power must have convinced him that everyone would be better off if she didn't have the ability to melt brains. Cookie seemed resolute. Farshad couldn't help but to admire her. Imagine having all that power and being willing to give it up.

He hadn't yet decided what he wanted to do. On one hand, having super strength could be amazing. If he learned how to really control his powers, he knew he could be unstoppable. But on the other hand . . . what if he couldn't control himself? What if he became like Mr. Friend, unstable and unable to stop himself from doing incredible damage? Farshad had already destroyed a computer keyboard and a phone and a kitchen counter and a car bumper, and there was no telling how much more he'd demolish, especially if his powers increased. And it seemed like everyone's powers were increasing.

Farshad looked over to where Willis was standing with Rebecca and Beanie. He, at least, was determined to get rid of whatever was causing his brain to run like an insane hamster on a million-mile-per-hour wheel. Rebecca, who could heal with lightning speed, wanted to return to normal as well, which seemed crazy to Farshad. He'd have loved to have that power. But she was convinced that by giving it up she would be welcomed back into her community. Farshad knew his parents would never have rejected him the way that Rebecca's had shunned her, but what if they did? Would he even want to go back to them?

Beanie had remained quiet about what he wanted to do. He could make himself as heavy and immovable as a rock, which seemed to Farshad like the sort of power that would be pretty easy to hide. Nick was going to try to keep his power, as was Abe, who really seemed to enjoy talking with animals and didn't seem particularly worried about being shunned if he was found out. Maybe a man's power to easily herd livestock was more important than a girl's power to heal herself.

"Okay, team," Jay addressed the group, rubbing his hands

together. "I wish I had time to think up a name for us but . . ."

"The Sprayers," Willis blurted.

"The Odd Army," Nick offered.

"The Oddballs," Cookie grumbled.

"The Antidoters," Kaylee suggested.

"Project Extreme Awesomeness," Kameron chimed in.

"Nerdapalooza," Kurt snickered.

"Terror Force One," Farshad found himself saying.

"Terror Force Fifteen," Martina added.

"The Goat Wranglers," Paul said, looking at Gertie.

"*Maah*. Feed me. Why are we standing here. Everyone is stupid," Gertie whined.

"The Sabotage Squad," Beanie said.

"Okay! Apparently we did have time to think up a name for us. The Sabotage Squad it is," Jay said, looking at Beanie with approval before turning to Nick. "Nick, old sauce, are you ready?"

Nick took a deep breath and held out his hand to Willis, who took it with a wild look in his eye. A split second later they were gone, and a few seconds after that Nick had returned to hold out his hand to Rebecca. "I left him in the women's bathroom, so you should probably be next?"

One by one Nick transported the Sabotage Squad except for Abe and the Farm Kids into Auxano's underground-lab-wing women's room, ending with Gertie. "*Maah*," she said, "I was there and now I'm here. I don't like it."

"Shhh!" Jay hissed, shooting a frustrated look at the goat. "We'll get caught!"

"But I'm hungry," Gertie pointed out.

Abe grabbed some paper towels and gave them to Gertie to eat, which immediately quieted her down.

"That was close," Jay breathed. "We're going to have to be more careful if we're going to get this done. Okay, Sabotage Squad, into your teams." The group shuffled around in the crowded bathroom and Farshad found Martina and Nick by the handicapped sink. He could feel his heart pounding in his chest. This was really happening. They were really going to do this crazy thing. He looked to his friends and felt a strange surge of comfort. At least they were doing this crazy thing together.

"Are we all ready?" Jay asked the assembled groups.

"Yes!" they whispered back in unison.

"What . . . what are you all doing here?" A woman in a lab coat who had just entered the bathroom gasped. "Is that a goat?!?"

"Mom!" Jay yelped.

"Yes, I am a goat. Give me food," Gertie bleated.

**EANIE WAS THE FIRST TO MOVE, QUICKLY STEPPING** to block the door to keep Jay's mom from leaving the crowded bathroom. Nick could see that Dr. Carpenter knew she was trapped.

"What is going on here?" She turned to her son. "Jacob Hieronymus Carpenter, what are you doing here?"

Nick had only ever heard Dr. Carpenter refer to Jay by his full name one time, and that was when they were seven and Jay had built a pair of wings out of a shredded feather pillow held together with wax from cheese rounds and was about to jump off the Carpenters' roof. Showing up in the ladies' room of her secret underground lab with a bunch of kids and a goat was probably worse.

"Now, Mom," Jay started.

"Nick, is that you?"

"Hi, Dr. Carpenter." Nick felt his cheeks getting red with embarrassment and wanted to be anywhere other than—

He was back in front of his old house. "No!" he heard himself crying out. "Not here!" He had to get back to help his friends. He really, really didn't want to but he had to—

"Nick!" Abe yelped before Kaylee and the Farm Kids shushed him from their spot at the edge of the forest.

"Is it time for Operation Chaos already?" Paul asked, and before he could answer Nick found himself back in the women's bathroom.

"AAAAUUGH!" Dr. Carpenter screamed.

"Nick! You weren't supposed to let anyone see that! What are we supposed to do with her?" Cookie asked in a panicked voice.

"Can you all do that?!?" Dr. Carpenter asked, her voice quaking.

"Don't answer her!" Jay belted. "Don't tell her anything! For all we know, she's part of this!"

"Oh, she is definitely part of this," Cookie said, shooting a look to Nick.

"What? What aren't you telling me?" Jay looked wildly at Nick, who was struggling to calm down and remain in one place.

"I may have forgotten to mention to you that it looks like your mom is in charge of this whole project," he said quietly.

Jay stared at Nick with his mouth hanging open.

"I'm really, really sorry," Nick said, staring at his feet and willing them to stay where they were, "there just never seemed to be a good time—"

"Okay, enough," Jay said, and threw back his shoulders. "When all this is over we are going to work on our communication." He looked around the room. "Nothing has changed. The plan remains the same. Only, now it looks like we have to lock my mother in the bathroom."

"Jacob Hieronymous Carpenter!"

"Sorry, Mom. Sabotage Squad, deploy!"

The different teams ran out into the hallway. Beanie was last, and after they'd shut the door on Dr. Carpenter, Farshad pushed his thumb into the doorknob, squishing it into uselessness.

"Sorry, Mom!" Jay said through the door.

"Jay, I—" Nick started again as they were about to part— he with Farshad and Martina and Jay with Willis, Rebecca, Beanie, and Cookie.

"Don't worry about it, old warthog, we'll deal with it later. But let's try to tell each other things in a timely manner from this point forward so there are no nasty surprises, okay?"

The sounds of alarms began to fill the hallway.

"I think I may have accidentally caused Abe and the Farm Kids to prematurely attack Auxano," Nick said.

COOKIE AND TEAM FORMULA FOUND THE LAB FASTER than they'd expected, and Beanie used his battering ram of a body to force open the door. Inside they'd found a small team of four bleary-eyed scientists looking up at them with confused terror.

"HELLO, SCIENTISTS," Jay shout-snarled. "My name is Jay but you may call me LASER EYES because I can shoot lasers out of my eyes and if you don't want to experience what that's like I suggest you all get into that supply closet right now."

The scientists must have seen some strange things over the course of their employment at Auxano because without any objections they all filed into the closet, which Beanie then blocked with a lab table that he'd ripped out of the floor by merely walking into it.

"I can't believe that worked," Cookie said, incredulous.

"Sometimes you have to come up with a story so preposterous that it has to be believed," Jay explained.

"So . . . your mom is going to kill you."

"Yeah, I am definitely in trouble."

"I'm really sorry about that," Cookie said.

"Me too," Jay said. He looked like he didn't want to talk about it, and Cookie felt a surge of gratitude for her mostly normal mom.

Outside the room Cookie could hear the alarms continue to go off, and she watched as Willis scurried around the lab, gathering materials with intense focus. It seemed completely bonkers to be leaving all of this up to a kid who seemed . . . completely bonkers, but he appeared to be confident in what he was doing. A lot was riding on him. Cookie watched as he poured precise mixtures of chemicals into vials for the massive centrifuge.

To the centrifuge room—

"They're coming!" Cookie said, panicked. Willis ignored her and kept mixing, but Beanie ran to the door and blocked it with his body right before the Auxano security team began trying to beat it down. But Beanie was immobile. Rebecca looked at his grim face and started to cry.

"How much longer?!?" Cookie asked as the thumping grew louder. It was as if instead of opening the door they were trying to obliterate it, and Cookie had no idea how much Beanie could take.

Cover your ears. That was Martina.

"Cover your ears!!! Do it now!" Cookie shouted, and stuffed her fingers into her ears right before the screaming began, first from the bunnies and then from the security forces outside the door. The pounding stopped.

Let me in, let me in!

"Let Martina in!" Cookie screamed to Beanie, who had his hands over his ears. She gestured furiously to the door with her foot, and after a moment of bewilderment Beanie cautiously moved away. Martina scrambled in with an armful of noise-canceling headphones and behind her Cookie could see Auxano security guards in fetal positions on the floor and holding their ears as fluffy screaming bunnies went hopping up the hallway.

Martina passed out the headphones and Cookie felt a surge of relief as she put them on. Rebecca put a pair on Willis as he started pouring his mixture into the spray bottles they had brought. "WE SHOULD SPRAY THOSE BUNNIES!" Cookie screamed before realizing that of course no one could hear her. She ran to the whiteboard and scribbled, *Let's spray the bunnies!*

Willis was working with complete intensity as if he'd spent his entire life working in that lab, and it occurred to Cookie that once he was cured all that scientific genius would be just . . . gone. He'd be an Amish kid again, educated in a one-room schoolhouse and expected to run a farm or maybe make furniture or saddles or something, and that would be it. If the antidote worked, then all his potential for incredible, maybe helpful discoveries would be snuffed out in an instant.

(But then again he would no longer be writing chemical equations on the walls.)

There were two spray bottles full of the antidote. Jay

grabbed one and went charging out into the hall. *Stay here!* he mouthed to Cookie before shutting the door behind him, and she and the others crowded around the little window in the door to watch as he chased the sonic bunnies down the hallway.

THEY SEEMED TO HAVE LOST MARTINA, BUT FARSHAD was strangely unworried. Maybe it was because she always seemed to land on her feet, or maybe because they were surrounded by blaring alarms and flashing lights, and in all honesty he was more worried about not running into Auxano security forces while trying to break out a bunch of feral middle schoolers and a dude who could make fires so that they could hopefully be sprayed with an untested antidote. Martina was probably fine.

Nick was in the hall in front of him, leaning against each door they passed, transporting himself into it, and then out again. "Another empty lab!" he called to Farshad, who was tall enough to peer through the small window in each door.

"This one's just an empty room," he told Nick, who rushed back to him before disappearing. Farshad looked into the window and saw him on the other side. Nick let out a sudden scream and jerked around.

"NICK!" Farshad shouted, and a moment later Nick was next to him again in the hallway.

"Look who I found!" Nick said excitedly.

"Hi, Farshad," a voice said, and Farshad turned around wildly, trying to see who it was until he felt a hand on his shoulder. "Don't be frightened," the familiar voice said, "it's

Ed. I'd shake your hand, but I'd rather not risk getting mine broken."

"Are you okay?" Nick asked. "Do you know where the others are?"

"Who, the substitute teacher?" Ed asked.

"Yes, and there are others."

"How many others?"

Over the sounds of the alarms Farshad heard a sort of dull roar. He felt a chill as the hairs on the back of his neck stood up. He'd heard that before. He pointed down the hallway. "Those others!"

They didn't have to look for the Company Kids; the Company Kids had found them.

"RUN!" Farshad yelled. Nick disappeared.

"Did you see that?!?" Ed screamed.

"GAAAARRRR!" the crowd of Company Kids screamed. They looked as though they had been sedated, but whatever they'd been given wasn't exactly working because they were clearly able to lurch toward them. Leading the charge were the Company Kids who had escaped from the overturned van—they, too, had come to save their friends. It would have been kind of sweet if Farshad wasn't terrified of them ripping him limb from limb.

"FORGET ABOUT NICK," Farshad screamed, "RUN!"

That's when they heard the first explosion.

**AY!!!" COOKIE FOUND HERSELF SCREAMING. SHE'D** felt at least four explosions since he'd run out of the lab with the spray bottles. She turned to Martina. "IS JAY OKAY?"

Martina looked at her, wide-eyed. Cookie carefully took off her noise-canceling headphones. There were no bunny screams. "Did you feel that?"

Martina took off her headphones, too, and this time they heard the explosion.

"ARE THE AUXANO PEOPLE THROWING BOMBS?" Cookie screamed, aghast.

Beanie rushed to the door and peeked out the window. Cookie could see strange blue smoke filling the hallway outside. "I can't see anyone," he said.

"What about Jay?" Cookie asked, panicked. She looked to Martina and was dismayed to see that she, too, looked frightened. "What do you see?"

"Nothing!"

"Wait, did it work? Are your powers gone?" Cookie asked, her voice trembling. Martina's eyes quickly shifted from brown to gray to a startling green. "No, no, you're still normal. Or . . . normal for you."

"Okay, done!" Willis said, putting the caps on the remaining spray bottles.

"What do you mean, done?" Rebecca asked.

"The formula. It is done now."

Cookie turned to stare at him. "Was it not done before?"

"No."

"THEN WHAT DID JAY JUST USE TO SPRAY THOSE BUNNIES?"

Willis looked at her blankly.

"The Company Kids are out! They've escaped!" Nick suddenly appeared next to Rebecca, who let out a little shriek.

"What do you mean, they've escaped?" Cookie asked.

"I thought we wanted to get them out so we could spray them," Martina added.

"We can't spray anyone!" Cookie yelped. "I think the spray is making people explode!"

"I would rather not explode," Beanie chimed in.

"Wait, what? The spray doesn't work?" Nick asked.

"It will work," Willis said.

"I'M PRETTY SURE ABOUT FIVE BUNNIES JUST EXPLODED FROM THAT SPRAY!" Cookie shrieked. "AND JAY WAS WITH THEM AND WE CAN'T FIND HIM."

Nick's eyes widened in fear. "What? What's happening? Where's Jay?"

"He went out— No!" Cookie cried, launching herself at Nick. "You can't go out there, the hallway is full of some sort of chemical mixture that makes screaming bunnies explode!" She grabbed hold of his arm to stop him, and suddenly they were back in the women's bathroom.

"Dear god!" Dr. Carpenter bleated. "Nick! You . . . Nick!"

The alarms were still blaring, but Cookie could hear the sounds of a crowd of . . . people? Dogs? outside making their way through the halls. Dr. Carpenter rushed to the door. "HELP!" she screamed, banging on it with both fists. "I'm in here, help me!"

"No no no no no no no!" Nick said, looking at Cookie. "It's the Company Kids!"

"HELP! SOMEBODY LET ME OUT OF HERE!"

There was a massive bang on the door—someone on the other side had heard Dr. Carpenter and was trying to get in. Cookie watched in horror as the heavy metal door began to buckle from the force of the banging.

"Let . . . me out of here . . ." Dr. Carpenter whimpered.

Cookie grabbed Nick with one hand and Dr. Carpenter with the other. "Get us out of here!"

And then they were in a darkened house. It smelled slightly of smoke.

"What . . . where . . ." Dr. Carpenter looked around wildly. "Nicholas, are we in your house?"

They had landed in his kitchen. "I'm sorry, I guess I just felt like we needed to get somewhere safe . . ." Nick said, looking around.

"Did *you* do this?" Dr. Carpenter looked aghast. "How . . . No, we need to get you back to the lab right now . . ."

"Why, so you can do experiments on us, I mean, him?" Cookie asked, suddenly angry.

"No, no, of course not, we just want to help him," Dr. Carpenter quickly said.

"What, like you helped Mr. Friend?" Cookie took a step toward Dr. Carpenter, who cowered a little. "Like you helped those kids to get better test scores?"

"We didn't mean . . ."

"You didn't mean to WHAT? Look at Nick's house! YOU. DID. THIS."

"Cookie," Nick said, "Mr. Friend did this . . ."

"Sure, but would he have had the power to start random fires had this crazy lady not decided that it would be a swell idea to play with people's brain chemistry so that some kids could get smarter?" Cookie asked.

"We never intended . . ."

"THEN WHY DID YOU GIVE THE COMPANY KIDS THE FORMULA?" Cookie found herself screaming. "You knew what it did to Mr. Friend but you gave it to them anyway. You gave this stupid formula to kids who already had smart parents and all the opportunities in the world because somehow that wasn't enough so you had to make them into total freakshows and FOR WHAT? So they could do well on tests?"

"Well . . ." Dr. Carpenter started. "Getting into a top college is very difficult . . ." Her voice trailed off.

"We've got to get back to Auxano and find Jay," Nick said.

"Oh, that's right, your son might be hurt from an exploding rabbit," Cookie snarled, and grabbed Nick's hand, and they were back in the Auxano women's bathroom.

It looked as though the door to the bathroom had been ripped entirely off its hinges, and signs of the Company Kids' destruction was everywhere. The hallway was filled with smoke. In the distance Cookie could hear barking, which she really didn't want to think about.

"JAY!" Nick yelled, trying to see through the smoke. Cookie opened her mind to search for the sound of Jay's thoughts, but all she could hear was the dull, dumb pandemonium of Company Kids' thoughts.

"RUUUNNNN!!!!" a voice shrieked, and Cookie watched in astonishment as Jay and Farshad went flying by them. She looked at Nick and they raced after their friends.

"Jay, you're alive!" she yelped with joy.

"STOP!" Nick gasped, and held out his arms. Cookie, Jay, and Farshad ran back to him and he wrapped them all in a big bear hug.

"This is nice!" Jay said. "But we should probably go."

**H GOOD, YOU ARE HERE,"** WILLIS SAID. **"TIME TO** spray the goat and see what happens."

"What? No!" Farshad watched as Jay leapt in front of Gertie. "Willis, old man, your antidote is dangerous. It made little bitty, very loud bunny rabbits go all explode-y. We just have to find a way to get out of here."

Willis shook his head. "No, I am sure it is fine. Bring me the goat."

"Did you not see those bunnies exploding?!?" Cookie asked, horrified.

"No. I am pretty sure the antidote is fine. Bring me the goat. Please."

"I do not want to explode!" Gertie bleated.

"We can't kill Gertie!" Nick said.

"Help! Help! I do not want to explode!" Gertie looked wildly around for an escape route. "You are all terrible people who take me to strange places that don't have food and then you don't feed me and now you are going to blow me up! I disagree with this! I disagree!!!" And with that she started running around the room.

"Get him!" Rebecca cried as Gertie darted in and out between everyone in the room and knocked over lab equipment.

"She's a girl!" Willis said, chasing Gertie with a spray bottle.

"MEH! MEH! I DON'T WANT TO BLOW UP! YOU ARE ALL TERRIBLE PEOPLE!"

"Watch out!" Farshad yelled. "If you spray the wrong person we'll lose our powers!"

"OR EXPLODE!" Cookie added, hiding behind an over-turned lab table.

"No one will explode, no one will explode," Willis gasped, trying to corner Gertie.

"What about the bunnies?" Nick asked.

"That wasn't my formula! I'm pretty sure," Willis said.

"Then why did they explode?"

"Probably because of him," Martina said, pointing to the now-open door.

It was Mr. Friend.

"I can't control it!" the substitute teacher shrieked as smoke billowed in from the hallway behind him.

"SPRAY HIM!" Cookie shouted.

"Who's he?" Willis asked.

"NOT ME!" Gertie bleated.

"WE HAVE TO GET OUT OF HERE!" Nick yelled, throwing his arms around Martina, who in turn grabbed Farshad's hand. Farshad suddenly felt the pressure of another body colliding into him, and the next thing he knew they were all slipping and falling on wet grass near the edge of the forest that surrounded the Auxano campus.

ICK HAD MANAGED TO GRAB MARTINA AND Farshad, but to his surprise Cookie had grabbed hold of him as well, and they all tumbled together into a pile at the edge of the forest.

In the distance they could see smoke pouring out some of the windows of the Auxano building, and they could still hear the alarms going off. There was a huge smoking hole in one of the outer concrete walls, and Nick couldn't tell if someone had used it to get in or out of the building.

"That does not look good," Martina observed.

"We have to get back in!" Farshad gasped. "We can't just leave Jay in there to fight by himself!"

"If we go back in, we'll breathe in the spray and lose our powers," Cookie said.

Nick looked at her, confused. "I thought you wanted to lose your powers," he said.

"I . . . I think I've reconsidered? I can't make this decision right now," she said, her voice miserable.

"Screw the powers!" Farshad said. "We need to help Jay!"

Nick turned to Cookie. "Can you hear him? Can you hear what's going on in there?"

Cookie closed her eyes. "It's just kind of chaos." She turned to Martina. "What about you?" she asked her. "Can you see anything?"

Martina trained her eyes on the Auxano buildings and in

the moonlight Nick could see her eyes turning a startlingly light green. "I see a building," she said.

"Thank you, Captain Obvious," Cookie growled. "Now is not the time for your patented Martina weirdness."

"I'm still looking," Martina said. "I see a building and I don't see anyone coming out of it. There are lots of doors and a big hole in the wall, but everyone is staying inside, even though parts of it are on fire."

Nick looked at the building. If they went back in, they could get Jay and the others out. If they didn't, they'd keep their powers.

It wasn't worth it.

"I'm going back," he said. "Who's with me?"

"I am," Farshad said.

Cookie looked resolute. "Me too." She took her sweater off and wrapped it around her face.

Martina did the same and picked up a big stick. "I'm ready."

"What, are you bringing a weapon?" Nick asked.

"You're not?"

"Let's go through the hole," Nick said. "I don't want to go back to the women's bathroom." He grabbed his own stick and they set off running down the hill toward the building they'd just escaped.

"FOR JAY!" Farshad yelled.

I T WAS STILL SMOKY IN THE HALLWAY WHEN THEY RE-entered the building, and Cookie immediately took off her sweater and tied it around her face. Martina saw her and did the same. Farshad used his thumbs to rip the sleeves off of his hoody and gave one to Nick. They looked like nerdy banditos.

"AAAAAAAAAAHHHH!!!" The screaming was coming from somewhere nearby, and Farshad led the charge toward the noise. They turned a corner to find Jay, naked to the waist and running at them with two half-full spray bottles of formula. "AAAAAAAAAAHHHH!!!"

"Jay!" Nick yelled, "It's us!"

Jay stopped short. "The cavalry has returned, splendid!"

"What happened to your shirt?" Cookie asked, eyeing Jay's skinny white chest.

"It was covered in rabbit entrails, so I took it off. I am probably deeply and irrevocably traumatized! But no matter, Willis's antidote works!"

"How do you know?" Farshad asked, just as Addison came barreling around a corner. Her hair was wild and she was screaming incoherently. Jay leapt in front of the others and began running toward her while misting her with the spray bottles. She screamed and dropped to the floor.

"Addison!" Cookie found herself shrieking.

"Bluuurrrgggh," Addison groaned from her place on the floor. They heard a nearby explosion. Jay knelt down beside the fallen girl.

"My dear!" he yelled over the alarms and other nearby screams. "You're going to go with Cookie!" He turned to Farshad. "Can you lift her?"

Farshad ran forward and scooped Addison up as if she weighed nothing. "Take her to the lab with the others!" Jay yelled. "And find a way to get out of here!"

"What about you?" Cookie asked.

"I've got work to do," Jay said grimly, wiping the sweat and soot off his forehead with his skinny forearm before dashing off down the hallway.

"Maybe he's looking for more Company Kids?" Cookie asked.

"And Mr. Friend," Martina added. Right. There was still a crazy fire-thrower in the mix. GREAT.

The smoke was getting thicker and Cookie started to cough. "We have to go!" She turned to Nick.

"I'll get him," he said, jogging down the hall after Jay.

Cookie and Martina followed Farshad as he ran with Addison away from the heat. Auxano was a mess—there were scorch marks everywhere, as well as smoke and debris. Cookie slipped on what looked like—was that poop? Was that *animal* poop? Martina grabbed her hand to keep her from falling and they kept running until they got back to the lab where Willis had created his antidote.

In it they found a crowd of people. In one corner the Company Kids were huddled together, and in another Beanie, Rebecca, Willis, Abe, and the Farm Kids were eyeing them warily. The team of chemists had been let out of the closet and were tending to all the crying kids, Gertie the goat had her head in a garbage can, and there was a herd of . . . dogs.

"We've got to get out of here!" Cookie said. There was smoke in the lab, and it wouldn't be long before they were completely trapped.

"There's no way out!" one of the chemists said. "We're three stories underground."

Nick! Cookie thought desperately. *Nick, we're all trapped here!*

"Is everyone here . . . okay?" Farshad asked, looking from the dogs to Abe to Beanie and Rebecca and Willis.

"Willis is, but Beanie and I are still . . . you know," Rebecca said. "Jay sprayed the goat, and she immediately stopped talking. Then he sprayed Willis, but that's when the explosions began and he went running off with the sprays, and then Abe came in with all these dogs. Do you know how to get out of here?" she asked.

"The hallway is filled with smoke," Farshad said.

"Nick . . ." Cookie began, and suddenly he was right next to them. "Nick! We've got to get everyone out of here!"

"Right . . ." Nick said, looking around wildly at everyone. "I'm pretty sure we have to go in small groups, I can't get everyone out at once and I still have to find Jay . . ." He disappeared.

The room was getting hotter, and nearby an explosion sounded. One of the scientists started to whimper.

Farshad whipped his head around in search of an escape route. "Even if Nick gets back, there's so many of us. We can't wait for him to transport each and every one of us." He looked at his thumbs.

"Could you use those to bust through a wall or something?" Cookie asked in desperation.

"We're underground," Martina pointed out.

"Does anyone have any ideas?" Cookie looked at the groups of crying Company Kids, terrified Farm Kids, and the chemists.

"I do," Rebecca said. She looked pale and extremely grim. "We walk out." She looked at Beanie. She ran to the door, wincing with pain as she opened it.

For the first time Cookie could actually see the fire, and it was terrifying and very, very hot. Rebecca walked right into it.

"NO!" Farshad yelled, lunging after her. Cookie and